D0895132

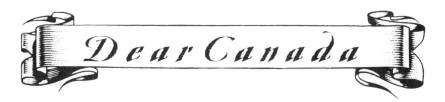

FLAME AND ASHES

The Great Fire Diary of Triffie Winsor

BY JANET MCNAUGHTON

Scholastic Canada Ltd.

St. John's, Newfoundland, 1892

Friday, June 3, 1892

Everyone knows it's bad luck to set sail on a Friday, but I spent a good bit of the week embarking on this project, so starting this diary today shouldn't jink me. At least, I hope it won't. Perhaps I should begin by recording how I came to be writing an Account of My Life in this painfully plain ledger book.

I would not have chosen to keep a diary. The decision was made for me by Miss Cowling and, I allow, by Alfie's India rubber ball. If I had left that ball at home where it belonged, if I had not been so close to the school when I tried to discover how high it would bounce, and if the wind off the harbour hadn't chosen just that moment to gust up a gale, I'd never have found myself sitting in the principal's office. Miss Cowling is much nicer than Miss Bolt (who cannot abide a fidget in her classroom and feels compelled to tell me so at least once a day). Our principal is generally patient and kind, but I could see that the Incident of the India Rubber Ball had brought her to the end of patience.

"Tryphena," she began with a sigh, "whatever shall we do with you?"

I know I'm in for trouble when anyone calls me by my full name. I told her I'd pay for the damage if she named the sum. (Papa is very generous with pocket money.)

When she agreed, I thought I was out of the woods, but then she said, "Poor Miss Bolt is at her wit's end with you."

It seems to me that Miss Bolt's wit ends much sooner than it ought to, but before I could get myself into even more trouble by saying so, I was struck with the fear that Miss Cowling would speak to Mama, and I knew the terrible punishment that awaited me if she did. Mama has been threatening me for weeks now with Proper Playmates — girls who can sit still for hours at a time and make polite conversation, who never tear their dresses climbing trees and never play pirates with their little brothers. Once I began to confide in Miss Cowling, I couldn't stop. I'm afraid, in the heat of the moment, I may have gone so far as to tell her I was quite certain I would die if I couldn't play with Alfie anymore. Finally she held both hands up to silence me, telling me to calm myself and asking why it's so important for me to play with Alfie.

I explained that Alfie should have started school last year when he turned seven, but Mama and Papa held him back because he has a weak chest and the diphtheria has been, as Nettie would say, so wonderful bad. (I allow I would never have learned how to spell the word *diphtheria* if it hadn't ruled our lives these past three years.) I told her Mama has been afraid to let Alfie play with other boys his age, so I am his faithful companion.

Miss Cowling smiled and said that was an admirable role for an older sister and she would not wish to be the cause of parting me from Alfie. Then she said, "What you need, my dear, is a project to teach you patience."

This pleased me because I already have one on the go. I'm more than halfway through a piece of Fancy Needlework. I painted the picture myself. It's an old-fashioned mourning piece, with a willow tree and a woman dressed in black leaning on a pillar topped with an urn. Nettie Sweetapple, our housekeeper, advised me on the design and she pronounced it "right tragical and romantic," which is high praise from her indeed.

I didn't tell Miss Cowling that I hope to have the piece all clewed up for our school closing ceremony next month, so it can be displayed along with the Fancy Needlework done by all the other girls. I am keeping this a secret, hoping to surprise everyone (and I think it will, because Miss Cowling was doing her best not to act too surprised to learn I could sit still long enough to embroider anything).

Sadly, she then asked how my needlework was progressing.

Sometimes, I wish I could lie. Everyone says honesty is a virtue, but it is often a trouble as well. I had to admit that needlework's much harder than drawing. "If my attention flags, even for a moment, the embroidery silk is all tangles. But," I added, "I am determined to make a good job of it."

Miss Cowling thought for a moment, then she took a small book from the bookshelf by the window and placed it on her desk between us. It was her diary, and she told me she had been keeping one since she was my age.

It was the most beautiful book I had ever seen — bound in red leather with gold tooling — and I told her so. If I'd known what she was planning, I wouldn't have made so free with my thoughts.

Miss Cowling said a diary would be a fine project for me. It would help me to sit still, teach me patience and might even improve my Fancy Needlework. The way she went on, anyone would think keeping a diary would cure all the World's ills. Finally she said that if I promised to keep a diary — and pay for the damage I caused, of course — she'd see no need to draw the Incident of the India Rubber Ball to Mama's attention. Though she will never read my diary, she said she will, from time to time, ask me to report how many pages I've written.

Well, I'd walked right into that. I had to promise to keep a diary most faithfully. But I left her office smiling all the same, as I also escaped the terrible punishment of Proper Playmates.

Saturday, June 4th

Before I could begin to keep this diary, I needed a book to write in, of course, so my first task was to raise the matter with Mama. My chance came on the very day Miss Cowling had extracted the promise from me, while Alfie and I were playing in the kitchen after school. I am probably too old to spend so much time in the kitchen now that I am eleven and almost a young lady (as everyone keeps telling me), but Alfie loves to play there, and as Mama says, wherever Alfie is, I can generally be found as well. We do get under foot, but Nettie never complains. I would say Alfie is Nettie's special pet, but Alfie is everyone's pet.

Mama came downstairs to talk to Nettie about a supper party she and Papa are hosting next week. I waited very nicely until Mama finished discussing the menu with Nettie before I spoke, just to prove to myself I *could* be patient if I'd a mind to be.

"Mama," I began, "I have decided it would be Improving for me to keep a diary." Mama is very fond of Improving Projects and I could tell at once by her smile that she approved. I'm afraid this success went right to my head as the image of Miss Cowling's beautiful little diary sprang to mind, and I made the mistake of asking for one just like it. "Do you think Papa could find such a book?" I ended.

But the smile had already fallen from Mama's face. "Tryphena Winsor, if I hear you say the words 'red Moroccan leather' to your papa, or if a book of that description enters this house, you can expect to wear last summer's gloves all summer long."

This was most unfair. She knows last summer's gloves have a small mend at the base of the right thumb. I reminded her that my new summer gloves had already been chosen. We happened to be in the store when the new stock was put on display, and Phoebe Dewling, one of Papa's best shopgirls, helped me find just the perfect pair. (Then Mama made her put them away, so I wouldn't ruin them before summer began.)

"And I was planning to give last summer's gloves to Ruby as an Act of Charity," I told Mama to cap my case, because she is very strict about being kind to Ruby, and I *had* planned to. Really.

Mama told me I had better do as she wished if I expected to have my new gloves for the school closing ceremony. Then I had to listen while she explained to Nettie that I am now forbidden to go into the store without her because Papa likes to shower small presents on me if Mama's not there to stop him, and how I haven't the sense to say no as Sarah does. She went on until my ears burned.

Mama fears that Papa's presents will somehow ruin my character, but I'm sure she's got it backwards. I know that people fall prey to their baser instincts *because* they long for pretty things. Last winter, I saw a girl who was caught trying to steal a pretty fur muff at the skating rink and I feel quite certain she would never have done so if she'd had a papa who showered her with small presents. But there's no use arguing with Mama about such things. She was a Methodist until she married Papa, and I allow that accounts for her stern nature.

That evening, Mama asked Papa to bring home this ledger book for me to write in. Then Mama told me a diary is a private thing, and she would never read what I write, and she said I could lock it away in the top drawer of my dresser where I keep my strand of pearls.

This ledger came home with Papa yesterday and it's some ugly, bound in dark green canvas, with ordinary, lined paper. I allow the lines are helpful, and I should be grateful to have such a Useful Book, but it looks quite out of place in my beautiful bedroom. I was that disappointed, I could hardly bring myself to put pen to paper last night. Papa must have noticed how crestfallen I was, because today he brought me a wooden lap desk, most cunningly made and very beautiful. It closes into a carrying case with a fine brass handle and has a marquetry compass rose worked in different coloured wood. When open, there's a wooden surface for writing, a tray for pens, two crystal inkwells and a blotter. Mama frowned when she saw it, but I was so delighted and thanked

Papa so nicely she finally had to smile. Papa said it seemed made for me because he knows I wish to travel the world when I am grown. Now, though I may not have something pretty to *write in*, I do have something beautiful to *write upon*, which makes a world of difference.

There. That's the entire tale of how I came to be keeping a diary. Next time, I will make a proper start on what a diary ought to be: The Story of My Life and Times.

Monday, June 6th

My name is Tryphena Elizabeth Winsor, and I am in Class II at the Church of England Synod Girls' School. Our school is named for its building, the Synod Hall, which has white clapboard and a gabled roof with a lovely little bell tower. Upstairs, there's a theatre where plays and concerts are sometimes staged. We hold our Christmas concert there and that's where the school closing ceremony will be held in July when the prizes are awarded to the best students. (I am never one.) Behind us, facing the Cathedral, is a row of buildings also belonging to the church, though not nearly as pretty — the Sunday School Building, the red brick Girls' Orphanage, the Bishop's House and the Clergy House. The Cathedral itself is a most beautiful stone building, and the pride of our city. (The Catholics, of course, have their own grand cathedral to feel proud of, just up the hill.)

I am grateful that Papa sends me to the C of E Girls' School rather than one of those private schools for girls where they study useless things such as Deportment and Manners. In our school, we learn serious subjects such as Botany and Mapping and Geography, which will be useful when I travel the world.

Today I walked home with May Seaward, as we always do unless the weather is shocking bad. We'd love to walk along Water Street, but the crossing-sweeper boys (who do little or nothing for the money they demand) are very rude if they don't get a penny as we pass the corners they call their own, even now that the streets are dry and passable! So we favour Duckworth, which is just one street up from the harbour and almost as fine. It's not the most direct path home, but it lets us view all the glories of our grand city. On the way to Duckworth, across from the Cathedral, is the most romantic dwelling in the city, Ashton Cottage. It has a sloping front garden, a long, sloping roof, and a porch bedecked with white scroll-work. Today, I told May I plan to live there when I grow up. (Unless, of course, I run off to somewhere more exotic.)

Well before we came to the Commercial Hotel, we could hear the music of the grand new barrel organ belonging to Mr. Michael Power. May and I always put a penny in his cup because his story is so sad and affecting. He worked in the mine at Tilt Cove until he was blinded by an accident. When Mr. Power began to beg, he managed to find an old barrel organ, but it was so feeble and squeaky it could barely play. Last year, some Water Street businessmen, Papa among them, took up a subscription to buy him his fine new organ, which was shipped all the way from the United States. I always feel so proud to have such a generous papa whenever I see it.

There's a gap in the buildings on Duckworth where I can catch just a glimpse of Papa's store down on Water. Today May and I passed at the very moment when my sister Sarah went in the front doors. Sarah is allowed inside the store any time she pleases (unlike me) because she has set out to learn everything about the millinery arts. Though she's only fourteen, Sarah favours Mama in the seriousness of her nature. When she takes an interest in something, she sets out to learn everything about it. (Papa calls her his little professor.) She even has her own collection of silk and velvet ribbons, and feathers and flowers made of cloth or paper, and she'll spend an hour or two working with the milliners whenever she can. When the demand for new hats reached a fever pitch just before Easter, Papa was happy to let Sarah work with the milliners every day after school and Saturdays too. By Easter she was shaping hat foundations, which is difficult work. She even learned how to block buckram frames.

Sarah has no trouble sitting still whatsoever and she reads a great deal when she's not sewing. We are so unalike, I sometimes wonder if perhaps the midwife brought Mama the wrong baby when I came into the family. I especially can't understand why Sarah wants to spend so much time learning to make hats. Papa could buy her any hat in the store.

Alfie has been at my door for a good five minutes, asking me to come and play pirates with him. I told him I'd just written about Sarah in my new diary and I didn't want to stop until I wrote something about him as well, and I'd be with him now the once if he'd give me a few minutes. This impressed him greatly, so he's gone off to the kitchen to get provisions for the next voyage on our pirate ship, the *Golden Hind* (which is really the third-floor landing where we can see out the Narrows to the open sea).

Before Alfie left, I reminded him to *walk* to the kitchen. (He still coughs a little when he runs.) I also made him promise not to slide down the mahogany banister. Unlike the dumb waiter, which requires me to operate when Alfie gets inside, he can go down the banister alone. If he's going to get into trouble with Mama, I would rather be there so we can pretend it was my idea.

Alfie is the Light of Our Lives, and he would

be perfect, except for his weak chest. Last winter Mama was terrified he had contracted diphtheria, even though we keep him away from other children as much as possible. After a few days, Dr. Roberts assured us it was only a bad cold, but Alfie was sick for weeks. Papa could see I was worried and he knows, when Alfie was too sick to play last winter, I read him all the poems in *A Child's Garden of Verses* by Mr. Robert Louis Stevenson. To comfort me, Papa said that Mr. Stevenson was just the same as a child, and we mustn't worry too much about Alfie.

Alfie enjoyed the poems so much that Papa has ordered a copy of *Kidnapped*, also by Mr. Stevenson, and Alfie and I will read it together next winter, whether he is sick or not.

Now I really must go and hoist the sails on the *Golden Hind* before Alfie comes back.

Tuesday, June 7th

I am not sure keeping a diary is having an Improving influence on my sewing. I tangled the embroidery silk while trying to make a French knot on the collar of the lady's mourning gown last night and had to pull it out and begin over again. But I will persevere with this diary because of my promise to Miss Cowling, of course, but also because the story of my life is so very interesting.

Very few girls in Newfoundland can boast a better

life, I'm sure. My family, the Winsors, are leading members of the St. John's merchant class. (Mama would call this statement vainglorious and boastful, but I wrote it anyway because it's true.) My father is the sole proprietor of Winsor & Son, one of the best mercantile premises on Water Street. Papa is, in fact, the Son, but he keeps his father's name in the company out of respect for my dear, departed grandpa. I also think he hopes Alfie will join him someday, and then the company really will be Winsor & Son once again.

Our house sits on Gower Street just a few blocks south of Government House, where Governor and Lady O'Brien represent Her Majesty Queen Victoria in Newfoundland. I like to think we live in the shadow of Vice-Regal Grandeur. (Sarah told me, quite sternly, that we would be tormented endless if I ever repeated such foolishness outside the house. So now I only *think* the words to myself before I fall asleep at night.)

The house took two years to build. We just moved in last October. Papa spared no expense, as it is a showcase for all the beautiful things he sells. But if anyone had asked me what our house should have looked like, I would have added a front garden and a porch like Ashton Cottage, instead of fronting right onto the street just like all the other houses. If we'd only done that, it wouldn't be so easy for me to hear people talk as they pass by and I would never have had the misfortune to overhear the men talking yesterday as I sat by the open window where the light was best, working on my Fancy Needlework. When one of them remarked what a grand house ours is, the other replied, "Yes, my son, that's what they calls Windsor Castle," and they both laughed, most unkindly. So now I am burdened with this disagreeable secret, and I can't tell a soul because I'm sure it would hurt Papa's feelings very much.

I can certainly understand why people might envy our house. It has three storeys above ground and a fine, cozy kitchen in the basement. The front door and our large picture windows are filled with leaded glass, thick and bevelled, that casts rainbows everywhere whenever the sun shines through. (Mama says it is much more tasteful than stained glass.) Mama has a grand collection of art glass and pottery around the house that Papa is always adding to. Since we moved in, I've spent many hours sketching the patterns on the tiles and wallpapers. Sometimes it is hard to believe how beautiful our house is.

In the old house on Patrick Street, I shared a room with Sarah, but here I have a room of my own, with a four-poster, oak bed, and a canopy of blue and green jacquard silk with a matching counterpane. Sarah's bedclothes are pink and gold. Mama wanted sensible patchwork quilts, but Papa prevailed. I'm sure that princesses in England do not sleep in beds finer than ours. Alfie has a hammock in a corner of his room so he can pretend he has run away to sea. (Last winter, when he was so ill, I slept in that hammock for three nights in case he needed me.) His room faces the Narrows, and he has a brass spyglass mounted on a tripod.

We moved the spyglass to the *Golden Hind* today, so I can help Alfie learn to read the flags on Signal Hill, which are very important to the merchants. The signal men on Signal Hill use their spyglass to watch for new flags at the lighthouse at distant Cape Spear, and then they copy them on the mast on Signal Hill. That way, everyone knows which ships are bound for our harbour and the merchants can prepare their wharves. Papa will be pleased to know we've been using the book of flags he gave Alfie.

I know I am very lucky. I could easily have been born into a poor family like Ruby's. Next time, I will write the interesting story of Ruby and how she came from Trinity Bay to be our maid of all work.

Thursday, June 9th

This is Ruby's story. Writing it down will remind me how fortunate I am, I'm sure (even though some people are cruel enough to ridicule our house).

Ruby Parrott is twelve, only a year older than I am, but she's already working far from her family. The day she arrived, I laughed when she said she came from Scilly Cove. I wasn't making fun of her, only it seemed funny because Ruby isn't the least bit silly. Mama made me apologize, and then Papa told us the Scilly Islands are off the western coast of England. Many Newfoundlanders came from the West Country and Papa said we should not laugh at good old English names, so now I don't. Ruby is small but sturdy with pretty orange hair and freckles. She reminds me of the girl in a fairy tale who works very hard and has only her upright character to recommend her, but somehow manages to triumph over adversity.

I know how Ruby came to be working here in St. John's at such a tender age because May told us last December when a snowstorm detained our drawing master, Mr. Nichols. (His lessons cost extra, but Drawing is very popular, so everyone in our class takes them, except for Susie Verge, our Charity Girl.) We meet in the Principal's parlour because Mr. Nichols is a fine English gentleman who is treated as a Distinguished Visitor. It's a pretty room where Miss Cowling receives visitors (though I would sooner learn to draw in a place where good upholstery and fine carpets did not lie so near, just waiting to be smudged).

Miss Cowling had ordered a fire to be laid in the fireplace, and I was wearing a thick flannel petticoat under my red wool dress. The snowstorm caught everyone unawares and somehow we were left to our own devices for the afternoon. When we realized this, we took off our smocks and put the drawing easels away and pulled armchairs up to the hearth. It was very cozy and felt like a holiday. The first few blizzards of winter are always exciting. (They do fray the nerves by April.)

Although there are nine girls in my class, May is my only True Friend because the other girls are not always kind to me (except for Susie, who is mindful of her place and keeps very much to herself). I am the smallest, I do fidget and, as Nettie says, I am born to trouble as the sparks fly upward. The other girls can sit still all day long — even Susie, who comes from a family of paupers — while my arms and legs start to move before I know what they are doing. Whenever I fidget too much, Minnie McGinty will look at the ceiling and say, "I think Miss Clara Butler forgot to take her monkey," dragging the memory of that long-gone principal and her cursed pet back from beyond.

Then my cheeks burn and the other girls laugh, all except for Susie, who stares at the floor, and May, who frowns. Thankfully, May's frown is enough to make Minnie behave.

Miss Bolt often says that May and I are like chalk and cheese (which *might* have been funny the first time). I know which of us is the chalk. May is a paragon of virtue but I love her anyway. She is gentle and pretty with curly blonde hair and eyes that are actually sea green, and even though I terrified her when we were first at school, in Infants, she has never blamed me. She learns all sorts of Interesting Things from the servants who are her main companions, so that's how May knows what she told us on that snowy afternoon: every fall, girls like Ruby come to town to go into domestic service if their families haven't laid up enough food to see everyone through the winter. That way, no one starves to death.

Still, Ruby wasn't shipped off heartlessly. She came to us with the highest recommendation from the Anglican clergyman in Scilly Cove, and she was chosen especially for us by Miss Maude Seaward, May's maiden aunt. I allow that Ruby was lucky to land here, because Nettie is so cheerful and Mama has raised us all to be kind and polite to the servants, but she cried buckets anyway for the first few weeks last fall. She tried to hide it, but Alfie and I would find her out when we were playing. I hated to be a tattletale, but she was so very miserable that I finally told Mama, who promptly enrolled Ruby in the Girls' Friendly Society. So now, Ruby goes off once a week to the meetings with Mama and Sarah and she has been formally befriended by Amelia Purchase, who is in the class ahead of me. Ruby no longer cries, but she's never very happy either. I think this is unfortunate because she has a very pretty smile and all this frowning may ruin her looks, which will make it harder for her to make a Good Marriage when she's older.

(Nettie says no one will ever marry me if I don't start behaving like a Lady, but I told Alfie that doesn't matter, as I plan to marry a Pirate Admiral and then I will be a Pirate Princess, and I'll order my husband's pirates to lop the head off anyone who is crooked with me. Then I had to make Alfie take an Oath of Secrecy.)

It doesn't seem right to have someone as sad as Ruby living in our happy home. Today I slipped her a peppermint knob, which I always think of as a very cheering sweet. We are *very* good to her. Ruby is the same size as I am, even though I'm small for my age. Last Christmas I gave her my best old dress on Boxing Day, rather than put it into the box that Mama was giving to the Girls' Friendly Society (who would only have given it to someone just like Ruby in any case). Even if the cloth had an odd greenish cast, it was a good dress with lots of wear left in it. The worsted wool was scratchy, and it did chafe a bit at the cuffs and collar, but it was very warm. I am not sure Ruby was properly grateful for this Act of Charity. I think those who are unfortunate enough to be poor should at least have the grace to show gratitude.

I didn't intend to spend so much time writing about Ruby, though I must say it made me feel much better about "Windsor Castle." Now, I must get on with my Fancy Needlework.

Saturday, June 11th

I miss May on the weekends. The sad truth is, I can never see May socially, and it's my fault. This is especially sad for May because her life is spent among extremely pious grown-ups. Her grand-father is the bishop's chaplain, and her father is also a clergyman. Her mother, grandmother and Miss Maude, her maiden aunt, devote their lives to Good Works. (Some of their works are very good indeed. Miss Maude was the one who noticed how clever Susie was at the Springdale Street Mission School and arranged for her to come to our school with all her fees paid.) May has no brothers or sisters — not so much as a cousin to play with.

I know it would do May a world of good to have a nice wild romp with Alfie and me, but I dare not ask, for Mama still doesn't know that I was banished from May's house. I've managed to keep this secret from her for three long years. When we were eight and in Infants, in our first year of school, Miss Maude thought I might make a suitable playmate for May, and I was invited to Ordnance House. It's a large and gloomy edifice, easily as big as two houses, which belonged to the regiment when British soldiers were still garrisoned here. Now that the government owns it, the Seawards live there because May's mother, Mrs. Seaward junior, is the Premier's niece. (This is a topic of lively conversation among adults, but Mama has warned it would be very rude to ever mention it to members of the Seaward family.)

As soon as I stepped inside Ordnance House, I became sure that it *must* be haunted. It was a dark, mauzy April day with fog streeling in off the harbour, perfect for ghost hunting. All the senior Seawards were off on Missions of Mercy, so May and I were free to roam from room to room while I made up tragic stories to explain why ghosts *would* haunt the house. One I still remember involved the consumptive fiancée of a faithful English officer stationed here during the last war with the French. She died in England and now, I told May, she often appeared to walk the floors of Ordnance House in her wedding gown, her face shrouded in a veil of the finest Devon lace.

The wind was high and it howled right mournfully across the chimney pots. Sarah and I shared a bedroom then, and she had just finished reading *Jane Eyre* by Miss Charlotte Brontë aloud to me, so the story was fresh in my mind. (Sarah is forever reading stories about girls who are suddenly orphaned and have to make their way in the world alone.) I asked May, didn't she think that noise sounded like the faint lamentations of a tortured soul? And perhaps there was a mad woman living in the attic. I really didn't mean to suggest there *was* a mad woman living in May's attic, but she had not yet read *Jane Eyre*, so she didn't understand that my question was inspired by Literature.

It was a perfect afternoon. After a few hours, Mrs. Mercer, the housekeeper, called us down to the cozy kitchen for bread and molasses. When Mama came for me, she was quite put out to discover us alone with the housekeeper. Later, I heard her tell Papa that May appears to spend altogether too much time alone with the servants and the Seawards ought to remember Charity begins at home.

Unfortunately, May proved to have a delicate imagination. The very night of my visit, she began to have nightmares and could not be left to sleep alone. I never imagined my fancies might affect her this way. I was only hoping to amuse her as I do Alfie, who has never been frightened by my stories, even when he could barely talk. (I did not understand then how fearless Alfie is. He has always loved to visit the little mummified Eskimo baby in the museum in the top floor of the Post Office, whereas May won't set foot up there for fear of it.)

Late one night when May woke up crying, Miss Maude demanded to know why this was happening and the whole story tumbled out. Soon after, Miss Maude required May to tell me that I would not be invited back to Ordnance House.

For weeks I lived in fear that one of the Seaward ladies might tell Mama, but that was the year the Board of Health closed all the schools two months early because of the diphtheria epidemic. There was very little visiting of any kind that spring; we even stopped attending church for a time. When the schools reopened in the fall, everyone seemed to have forgotten that May and I had ever played together, but we are still the best of friends in spite of everything.

I should not like to give the impression that the Seawards never think of May's welfare. Miss Maude brings her to the Girls' Friendly Society, where she is companion to a deserving maid of all work her own age. But May says Jenny is so much older in her ways, so keenly interested in fashion and thoughts of marriage, they can scarcely find a common topic of conversation. I'm sure Ruby would have made a better companion for May.

(Sarah goes to the Girls' Friendly Society too, but Mama says I am not fit, as I would be likely to turn a gentle housemaid into a little pirate. I would rather stay home and play with Alfie anyway.)

Tuesday, June 14th

Miss Cowling called me to her office this afternoon, and was pleased when I told her how many pages I have already filled in my diary, but I had to tell her the project does not seem to be helping with my Fancy Needlework. She suggested that I not try to sew immediately after writing, so now I am getting up early to write before breakfast. Mama is so pleased to know I've taken to this ugly ledger that yesterday we finally went to the store for my new summer gloves.

Today I think I will describe Papa's store while it is still fresh in my mind. It's a wonderful grand store, so I may well run out of steam before I can describe it all.

Most of the buildings in St. John's are wooden clapboard, even fine ones such as ours, but only brick and stone buildings are allowed on Water and Duckworth Streets, where business is conducted. Papa says they made that rule after the Great Fire of 1846 to prevent the city from burning again, and they widened the streets too.

Winsor & Son is a grand, three-storey, brick building that takes up a full third of a block on the harbour side of Water Street. But we don't just sell goods in our store; things are made there as well. Near Papa's office on the third floor, in rooms with skylights where the light is best, the tailors and dressmakers have their workshops. I love to hear the whirring of the sewing machines as we pass by on our way to see Papa, but we never interrupt. Mrs. Millie Steele, the head tailoress, is a stern widow from Scotland.

The second floor is used for storing stock, but that will soon change. Coming down the stairs to the shop on the main floor, I always feel a thrill to see the varnished wooden counters where smartly dressed shop clerks and shopgirls wait on customers. Every kind of treasure can be found at Winsor & Son: fashionable clothing; hats and shoes for women and men and children; jewellery, watches and clocks; yard goods and lace; and of course the confectionery counter. Though many things are made in the store, the soaps and perfumes and jewellery are imported from England and America and even more exotic places such as Paris, France. Altogether, Papa employs nearly sixty people.

Sarah's favourite place, of course, is the millinery department, where all the pretty hats are made with felt cloth or straw braid and sheets of buckram, right before the eyes of our customers. Miss Rosy Noseworthy just became head milliner last year when Father's previous head milliner, Miss Mary Prosper, married a lawyer, Mr. French. Miss Rosy is only twenty-two. She was seventeen when she came to work for us, and her mother, who was a widow in poor health, died soon after. (Miss Rosy is so very much like one of the orphans in Sarah's books, I wonder if that's part of Sarah's fascination with hat making.) Miss Rosy often says, being an orphan, she must work extra hard. She's joking, but Papa says she is worth her weight in gold. She is a *modiste* of the highest order, and all the fashionable ladies come to her for their hats, even the wife of the Premier.

Three milliners work under her, and there are also two apprentices close to Sarah's age, Prudence and Patience. Papa jokes that Prudence is the most impatient girl he's ever met and Patience is utterly lacking in prudence. They try Miss Rosy's patience and she sometimes blusters at them, but she is too kind-hearted to let anyone go, and quite proud of her teaching skills. (I once overheard her tell Mama that she felt certain she could teach a chicken how to make hats.) They also provide Sarah with excellent gossip.

I've only described part of Papa's premises, but Sarah just asked me to hold a skein of yarn while she winds it up. I don't know how she can think of knitting now that winter's over!

Wednesday, June 15th

This summer, Papa plans to expand the shop and move most of the storerooms across the harbour into an old stone warehouse on the South Side. He inherited the building unexpectedly last winter when one of his father's oldest friends died, but the warehouse sat empty for many years while old Mr. Fraser declined. After the warehouse has been cleaned out, the jewellery, watch and shoe departments will move to the second floor and the displays of clothing and furniture will expand on the main floor. Papa's family actually lived in those very rooms on the second floor of the shop when he was growing up! It's hard to imagine such humble beginnings.

Now Alfie wants me to play with him. I told him to wait while I write just one more sentence, but it's going to be two. I planned to finish my description today, but that will have to wait until next time.

Thursday, June 16th

As pretty as the shop is, the most interesting things happen on the wharf side, in workshops with stoves and open flames and fire buckets everywhere, where the sharp, sweet smell of burnt sugar from the confectionery kitchen competes with coal smoke from the blacksmith's forge. The candy kitchen is filled with pots of boiling sugar syrup, and we never go near there except for the Christmas toffee pull, when everyone is invited in for the day. Most merchants do not make their own candy, but Nanny Winsor, who died before I was born, learned to make sweets in England. At first she worked alone, but in time she ruled over many women in the large candy kitchen. Winsor & Son is famous for penny candy and boiled sweets which are sold all over the island, and we are proud of the tradition.

Behind the candy kitchen, Mr. Bright, the tinsmith, and Mr. Sampson, the blacksmith, work with their apprentices. Mr. Matthew Bright is young to be a master of his trade, but he comes from a large family of tinsmiths in Trinity. Alfie once asked how old he was when he first started, and he replied, "I allow I've had my hand at it since I learned to walk." His shop makes tins for our candies, buckets and coffee pots, baking sheets and bread pans, cookie cutters and even tin stars and icicles and candle holders for Christmas trees. No one has ever seen Mr. Matt lose his temper. He sometimes teaches his apprentices skills by making little toys, so he often has a toy for Alfie or me. Once, he gave me a clever little coin bank shaped like the Customs House. I treasure it.

Mr. Matt and our blacksmith work together in perfect harmony, although they are as much alike as May and I. Mr. Oswald Sampson is just like the strongman in the Bible whose name he bears, with a booming voice and a handlebar moustache (though I'm not sure they wore handlebar moustaches in Biblical times). Much of the hardware that's sold in the basement comes from Mr. Sampson's forge, which is open to the harbour on one side because of the fire. Mr. Sampson is much sterner with the boys in his workshop, because the work is often dangerous, I allow.

Some shopkeepers board their employees in rooms above the shop, but Papa just keeps one room in case someone who's hired is new in town. Most of Papa's crowd board in houses or hotels, except for the ones who grew up in town and still live with their parents.

A few even own houses of their own. Mrs. Millie Steele has a neat little house on Maxse Street and Mr. Sampson has his own house near the edge of town, just off Merrymeeting Road, where he lives with a wife and two sons.

Behind the workshops is Papa's wharf, where ships are unloaded under the stern eye of Mr. Stabb, the wharf master. He was a sailor for many years and still wears gold hoops in his ears. The wharf is a dangerous place with winches that move heavy barrels and crates and we are sternly forbidden to go there without Papa. Even the men who unload the ships must be careful, and they know what they're doing. Alfie and I would never disobey Papa in the store. We are also a little fearful of Mr. Stabb, who seems very fierce.

There. I think my picture of the store is quite complete!

Wednesday, June 22nd

Describing Papa's store must have worn me right out. Whenever I thought about writing in my diary this past week there was always a more appealing task at hand, but sometimes Papa's store provides us with Interesting Conversations, so I'm taking up my pen again today to record what I learned at suppertime. Papa said he held Matthew Bright responsible for lost time because girls from all parts of the business were forever finding excuses to visit his shop, but I could tell he wasn't really angry. Mama said Papa should count himself lucky that Mr. Matt has such an upright character, because he could toy with the affections of as many girls as he pleased. Father replied he thought Mr. Matt's heart belonged to one young lady in particular, and that was sad because at last year's Christmas toffee pull, she would not even give him the time of day. Alfie wondered if perhaps the lady had no watch. Mama laughed and explained that Papa meant the lady didn't like Mr. Bright well enough to talk to him.

Then Sarah said, if Papa was talking about Miss Rosy Noseworthy, Mr. Matt should turn his attentions elsewhere. Mama was so surprised, she dropped the sugar tongs. "But Sarah, why do you say that?"

Sarah told us what she'd learned from Patience and Prudence last week, when Miss Rosy was upstairs matching some hat felt to a dress. Patience and Prudence began to talk about the bachelors in the shop — which are kindest, which the most handsome, and who would make the best husband. At that point, Papa frowned and told Sarah that he did not approve of such talk in her presence, but Mama waved his objection aside.

"It can be useful for young girls to exchange such opinions, Gregory." She nodded to Sarah, "Go on." Mama takes a keen interest in the lives of Papa's crowd, almost as if they were family.

Sarah told us they decided Mr. Matt would make the best husband because he is so cheerful and kind, but then Patience said it was right sad Miss Rosy had jilted Mr. Matt last fall.

"I had no idea they were keeping company. Did you, Gregory?" Mama asked.

Papa replied that it was his custom to take no interest in such matters. Then Mama asked the very question I wanted the answer to. "But why ever would Rose throw him over?"

Sarah had the answer. Patience said Miss Rosy started to move in a better circle once her friend Miss Prosper was engaged to Mr. French, and she met a young lawyer named Mr. Rupert Waldegrave.

"A Waldegrave!" Mama cried, "Why, that's a leading family."

Sarah told us that Prudence said, after Miss Rosy met Mr. Waldegrave, she began to say she'd never marry a man who worked in an apron and went about with his shirt sleeves rolled up, not even noticing the smudges on his face, and now Miss Rosy wants to marry someone who will take her to Paris so she can see the new fashions for herself. "It seems Miss Rosy has set her cap for Mr. Waldegrave," Sarah concluded, "but then we saw Miss Rosy coming down the stairs and that was that."

Mama shook her head. "Rose is aiming far above her station."

"But Miss Prosper married Mr. French, Mama," Sarah reminded her.

Mama explained that the Frenches came to Newfoundland penniless and worked their way up, but William Waldegrave was a governor of Newfoundland in the 1700s and his has been one of the leading families ever since. She felt certain that the Waldegraves would never permit Mr. Rupert to marry a penniless orphan. Mama must be right, but it shocked me to think that anyone might view Miss Rosy in that way. Mama grew quite indignant as she continued. "Matthew Bright may not move in the best circles, but he has a fine, upstanding character, and a man with a trade can always support his family. Rose should know better than to judge a man by the clothes he wears."

Then Mama told us she hoped, when it came to courting, Sarah and I would think of more serious qualities than fashionable clothing. I could see that Alfie was about to say something, perhaps about pirates, so I had to give him a gentle kick under the table to remind him of his Oath of Secrecy. I am sure Sarah will be sensible when she's old enough for courting, but what about me? I rarely look beyond appearances. Does that mean I am bound to make a poor marriage? Because, in truth, I know one day I will have to choose a husband who won't be a pirate. The thought of growing up is enough to give me a sick headache.

Saturday, July 2nd

Last evening Mama and Papa hosted a dinner party, so Alfie and I were allowed to eat our supper off trays onboard the *Golden Hind,* as I imagine real pirates do.

The third floor is terribly hot now, but at least it wasn't smoky yesterday, so Nettie was able to open the window and we caught a cooling breeze from off the sea. (Forest fires have been burning outside the city off and on over the past few weeks. Some days the smoke is so bad that Alfie must stay inside.)

We spent the whole meal planning our summer holidays. Our summers are often wet and cool, but it has been hot and sunny for weeks now. Mama lets Sarah and me sleep in our chemises, because we have no nightgowns light enough for this weather and Papa says the store is running out of muslin and seersucker. The plants in our back garden even need watering!

Today Alfie and I pretended we were slaves in Ancient Egypt, hauling water for the workers who were building the pyramids as we carried tin buckets up the back steps from the kitchen so Mama's new rose and lilac bushes could have a nice, cool drink. My pinafore got muddy, but for once Mama didn't mind. It's a very good idea to wear a pinny to protect my dresses, but why must they be white, the colour most likely to show stains?

This summer will be different for another reason. The diphtheria epidemic has finally ended! The Board of Health took Serious Measures, even removing people from their homes to fumigate, and placing police constables at the doorways of those who refused to move, and this seems to have worked. Last summer Mama refused to believe it was over, but now I am sure she will give us more freedom.

Today, I told Alfie that I'm going to ask Mama if we may have picnics at Rennie's River. If we can convince Sarah to come too, Mama is sure to agree, and we are allowed to wander to Bannerman Park by ourselves, as it's just two blocks away. Of course, we are already talking about the Regatta. They have set the date for August 3 this year, weather permitting, of course. I marked it on Nettie's kitchen calendar for Alfie. Winsor & Son always has a team in the rowing races, and last year they came second in the men's final. We can't wait to see what happens this year.

Alfie and I also hope for an excursion to Freshwater Bay, which is the nicest picnic spot anyone could imagine. Once you sail through the Narrows, every trace of civilization vanishes, leaving nothing but endless ocean and high rock cliffs. Sailing down the shore, you soon come to a sheltered cove with a little freshwater pond protected from the sea by a long, rocky barachois. This is Freshwater Bay. There are woods on either side of the barachois where Alfie and

I explore, and beach rocks to collect, but we must wait until August, when the blackflies and nippers are gone.

The old stone warehouse on the South Side is another point of interest. Though it's filthy and it needs to be cleared out, Papa said he will take Alfie and me across in a boat to see it one day soon. Alfie is almost beside himself with excitement. His cough is very nearly gone now. This will be a glorious summer.

Friday, July 8th

I am so ashamed. I have been sent to my bedroom without supper. The whole summer is ruined and it's all my fault.

I knew that Alfie barely fit into the dumb waiter last fall, and I knew he was growing, but somehow I failed to connect those two things as any sensible big sister ought. The dumb waiter isn't intended to be hauling little boys. It's what Papa calls "a labour-saving device." Nettie can open the door in the kitchen, put our hot food inside and use the cable to hoist it up to the dining-room pantry, saving her from having to carry trays of dishes up and down the stairs. I only put Alfie in the dumb waiter when Mama and Nettie were both out of the house, which seldom happens. No one ever forbade us to put Alfie in there, but I knew, if anyone ever thought about it, they would. And it was so much fun. We never did it over the winter, of course. Alfie was too sick.

Oh! Mouser just rushed into my room and rushed out again. I almost spilled the ink. The wind is so high today, the cat is galey. Whenever high winds make her rush around, Nettie says she has a gale of wind up her tail. Mouser is a very pretty cat with fluffy black fur and white socks and a bib. I wish she was a pet but she's a working cat who lives in the basement to protect the kitchen, so she's hardly tame and sometimes scratches. In the uproar I caused today, she got out of the kitchen. I should tell someone, but Mama is so angry, I'm afraid to leave my room.

To return to my Shameful Story, Mama was invited out for tea and Nettie was on her weekly trip to the grocer. Ruby had taken a chair into the back garden to darn socks in the shade, so I didn't even have to worry about her telling on us (and I don't think she would). I checked on Sarah and found her in her room, sewing velvet pansies onto her summer hat, so Alfie and I felt safe. We were pretending that Peter Easton, one of our most famous pirates, had come to kidnap Alfie, and the dumb waiter was the perfect hiding place. He fit in with only a little pushing and was fine on the trip up to the dining room, though I did notice, as I pulled the cable, that he was heavier than he had been last fall. Then, when I tried to get him out, we found he was wedged in tight.

As always, Alfie was brave. After a bit, he said I should leave him alone get himself free, and I tried, but it was too hard to stay away and he'd made no progress. I tried to pull him out by the leg, but he said that hurt. He was starting to pant so I tried pulling his arm, but I couldn't budge him. By then Alfie was turning red and wheezing, so I pulled harder.

I thought about how sick Alfie had been last winter, and I was that frightened, I started to scream. Ruby came first, then Sarah, who told Ruby to run to the kitchen for a glass of water for me. I wanted them to help Alfie, not me, but somehow, this only made me scream more. When Ruby returned with the water, Sarah very calmly dumped it on my head. The shock of it made me stop screaming.

Now we all turned to Alfie. I thought at first he was having some kind of fit, but, in fact, he was laughing because Sarah had drenched me. I could still hear the wheeze in his laugh though. Ruby looked things over and said, "I'll be right back." She returned with the drippings tin, where Nettie keeps the grease from cooking. "We can rub this all over Master Alfie's clothing," she said.

Sarah started to protest that this would ruin his clothes.

"Never mind that," I cried. "Just get him out before — "

I was going to say "before Mama gets back," but

that was exactly what happened. Mama walked in the door

Oh dear, there's the fire bell. Well, it's not surprising with all this hot, dry weather, but the firemen are very clever and we have a lovely steam engine. I'm sure they'll have the fire under control in no time.

Mama smeared cooking grease on Alfie where she could, and he popped out of the dumb waiter like a greased pig. (They let a greased pig run free at the Regatta every year and whoever catches it can take it home.) I would say he came out as neat as can be, but "neat" would not describe him at that moment. His sailor suit is ruined and he needed a good scrub.

Alfie was still wheezing, so Mama sent Ruby to fetch Dr. Roberts and then she turned the full force of her attention to me. She said I have been running wild for far too long. She partly blamed herself for encouraging me to spend so much time with Alfie during the diphtheria epidemic, but that's over now and playing with Alfie has not had an Improving Influence on me. The terrible punishment of Proper Playmates has arrived.

She said, this summer, I will learn to be a lady. From now on, she will take me visiting. When visitors come to call, I will be present in one of my best dresses. I will learn to sit through afternoon tea and make Polite Conversation. Worst of all, she will invite

Proper Playmates to the house for me. I asked if May Seaward might do, and she said not nearly. Mama has a whole list of girls in mind and her notion of play runs along the lines of sewing together. Finally, she said, if I fail to cooperate in any way, I can expect to be sent to Professor Danielle for dancing lessons next fall. This would be A Fate Worse Than Death. Professor Danielle runs the Royal Restaurant on Water Street. He is a fussy old bachelor, and I'm sure I'd never be able to please him.

This is no life for a future pirate princess. I burst into tears and told Mama I would rather work in the kitchen with Nettie and Ruby all summer. That's when she sent me to my bedroom without supper. So the holidays are ruined and it's all my fault. Those dreary visits and long days with Proper Playmates now stretch before me. Nothing can save me from this fate.

There's the oddest commotion in the street. It seems to be moving day for everyone. Carts full of furniture go by, all moving east. Some men are carrying hand barrows piled with household goods. *Now* someone is banging on the front door. I must have a look.

I just stuck my head out the window to find Mr. McAllister, the old Scottish bachelor who keeps Papa's books, looking very flustered as the door opened, not like himself at all. I smell smoke, but we've been smelling smoke for weeks now. I do hope the firemen got that fire under control. What if it reached Water Street? But even if it did, those fine stone and brick buildings would never burn.

Mama is calling for me to come downstairs and she wants me to bring *all my clean underclothes.* Whatever can this mean? I know a person should not grow too attached to underclothes, but I am very fond of my chemises, petticoats and drawers. Can Mama mean to give them all away to the poor —

Alfie says I must come, right now. He's opened my dresser! I must —

Bannerman Park, Seven p.m.

The city is in flames. Out of sight from here, down the road past Rawlins Cross, a hard wind blows the fire relentlessly toward the harbour. We can only hope that everyone at Papa's premises is safe, and the places we love do not catch fire before the conflagration is under control. People are gathering in the park because it's upwind and safe. It may be hours before we can go home again.

This is the strangest day of my life. I'm sitting on the hard, dry ground in the park with Mama and Sarah and Alfie. It's lucky Papa gave me this lap desk. I'd never be able to write, otherwise. Nettie has gone off to see what she can learn about the fire, and Ruby is nearby with Mama's good silver chest on her lap. Around us, hundreds of people sit just as we do, with whatever they could rescue when they rushed from their houses. Some have cartloads of stuff, but most, like us, have almost nothing.

Since this is such a momentous occasion, I will record the events of this afternoon. When Alfie and I came downstairs, Mr. McAllister was already gone. He'd left the message that Papa wanted us to leave the house and go to Bannerman Park so he would know we are safe and so he would be able to find us later, should the worst happen. Sarah told me Mama wanted our underclothes to wrap her wedding china. We all set to work wrapping dishes while I begged Sarah for more details. The fire was still far from Water Street, Mr. McAllister had said, but everyone was ready to defend our premises if necessary. Then Sarah told me Mama had just emptied a barrel of flour *on the kitchen floor,* and we could hear Mama and Nettie wrestling the barrel up the stairs. I'd already wrapped the teapot and cream soup bowls when Mama arrived. She took over and told us to go upstairs to each fetch a small valise filled with whatever we valued most, but to hurry and come back quickly. So we did.

I remembered Alfie's good brass spyglass was aboard the *Golden Hind,* so I ran up to the third floor to fetch it. And there, of course, I had to look out the window. I could see no fire, but the harbour was filled with smoke, pouring out the Narrows toward the open sea. Buildings block our view of the streets below, but there was a good deal of confusion in the harbour itself as ships left the north side looking for safer berths. Until that moment, I was sure Papa was just being extra cautious. But when I saw that even ships' captains thought the fire could reach Water Street, I fled as if my fear had chased me down to my room.

I hardly remember packing at all. When I came down the stairs, the house felt silent and empty, as if we had already abandoned it. Mama stood in the main hall, tucking her sapphire necklace under her blouse. It is far too glorious to be worn with every-day clothes. Then she looked around in a hopeless kind of way. How could we just abandon our beauti-ful house? Ruby stood there, calm and sad as ever, with a small carpetbag on her elbow and her arms wrapped around our silver chest. Nettie was carrying two valises and crying. Mama took a deep breath and squared her shoulders. "Never mind, Nettie," she said. "We're sure to be back here tomorrow morning, right as rain."

Then Sarah came downstairs with Alfie, his hair still damp from scrubbing, and Mama shooed all of us out the door. We had to wait while Mama and Nettie got the barrel of china down the front steps.

A gust of wind blew my hat off and I had to chase it. When I looked up, I could see along to the end of Gower Street where the slanted roof of our Cathedral disappeared every few seconds into the smoke that billowed down from above. Suddenly a big chunk of flaming debris sailed by in the wind, trailing flankers like the tail of a comet. It went so fast, I thought my eyes had tricked me, but then some smaller pieces followed. All the roofs are dry as tinder. What would happen if sparks landed on them? No one else had seen, and I found I couldn't tell them.

Mama finally took the big iron key that locks the front door from her purse, but Alfie began to shout, "No, no, you can't, Mama! Mouser is inside. If the house catches fire she will die." He would not be comforted and soon he was wheezing again.

Mama grasped him by the shoulders and told him firmly that he must stop so we could leave before the smoke came our way. When she saw this wasn't working, she went back up the stairs and opened the door. "Look, Alfred," she said. "Look at me." She only calls him Alfred at the most serious moments. Then she told him we would leave the door open so Mouser could escape.

Alfie nodded and was quiet, but Nettie didn't like this at all. She wondered about robbers, but Mama shook her head and said, "Alfie's health matters more to me than anything we own." Then we began to walk to the park, Mama and Nettie rolling the barrel along carefully between them. A few men driving empty carts passed us and I thought they must be going to fight the fire.

We soon came to the park and here we remain. The wind seems hotter and drier than ever, and so strong it flings dust at us from time to time. This is like a grim picnic without games or food, and people have brought the strangest things. A large lady is sitting near us with her small boy and nothing but a blue and white vase the size of an umbrella stand. It's almost as big as her child. She keeps looking in the direction of the fire and twisting her purse strings. There are hardly any men here. Like Papa, they must be

I put my writing down because Nettie came back with news. She told us the fire started about 4 o'clock in a barn on Freshwater Road belonging to a man named Timothy O'Brien, or Brien, or Byrne. The alarm was raised, but many of our firemen were outside town, busy with a forest fire. Those who answered the alarm soon discovered there was no water in the pipes. Nettie said it had been turned off for repairs at Rawlins Cross today. The water was turned on again, but sadly, it had not yet reached the pipes in the upper levels.

I remembered the glass of water Sarah dumped on my head and reminded Nettie that we'd had water.

She replied that she'd seen a notice in the newspaper yesterday, so she'd filled some buckets. Mama beamed. Nettie always takes care of small things like that without even mentioning them.

Then the woman with the little boy spoke. "Yes, the pipes was empty but there's a tank near to where the fire started. It should have been filled, but from what I heard when we was stowing our furniture, they was playing at putting out fires a few weeks ago and nobody filled her up again." Her eyes brimmed with tears as she told us how they had lost their "neat little house on Courting Lane, freehold land and all." She found her hankie, blew her nose and went on to tell us that they had managed to hire a cart as the flames approached, and their rescued belongings were now safely stowed inside the Anglican Cathedral. "No way, my husband said, any fire is going to breach those stout stone walls," she concluded.

While Mama and Nettie congratulated her, I felt a glow of pride. Of course our Cathedral will keep everything safe.

The lady seemed pleased, but added, "I kept this vase with me anyway. The only thing in the world I got to remind me of my mother now."

A boy with a pail and tin dipper came around selling water for a penny a cup. Mama frowned. Everyone had been drinking from that cup and she still lives in dread of diphtheria. She pried our barrel open and took out six of her best china tea cups. Then she told the boy she would hold them while he filled them up.

The boy mistook her reason. "It don't matter if you got your own cups, Missus," he said, scowling. "It's still a penny each."

I'd never heard anyone speak so rudely to Mama and I held my breath to see what she would say, but she only nodded. The world is upside down today.

Just as I drained my cup, I recognized one of Mr. Bright's apprentice boys, Leander Janes. He was leading Mr. Michael Power and I was happy to see they had his new barrel organ in tow. Some friends came to guide Mr. Power away and I saw him offer a penny to Len, who shook his head as he backed away.

I stood up and shouted, "Len, Len, over here!"

Mama told me to stop yelling like someone from Tank Lane (which is what she always says when I yell), but Alfie was already on his feet and running, and I explained to Mama while Alfie brought Len over that he would have news of Papa.

Unlike the water boy, Len stood in awe of Mama, turning his cap in his hands as he spoke. He told us there was no sign of the fire on Duckworth or Water yet, but the shop was closed and all hands were ready with buckets and barrels of water.

Then he painted a picture I could never have imagined for St. John's — the streets filled with panic and looters. He said it costs the world to hire a horse and wagon down there now, but Papa had the luck to find Mr. Morrissey, our usual cabman, with his Victoria cab. While they filled his carriage with a few valuables, Miss Rosy demanded space for a box of her best supplies.

"As we loaded the goods into his carriage," Len continued, "looters were waiting to snatch them out again, circling like a pack of wolves." He told us Mr. Morrissey had his buggy whip raised, but then Miss Rosy got all the girls to surround the cab while it was filled. Len smiled for the first time. "You should've seen her, Missus. She tore such a strip off those sleeveens, big men the lot of them. They slunk away like dogs with their tails between their legs."

Then Len told us those looters had likely gone off to find another shop to pillage. We all protested that this could not be so, but Len stood firm. "Shops that stayed open are completely gutted now," he told us.

Len had met one of Macpherson's clerks when he was walking poor Mr. Power here and learned that the Constabulary had made everyone abandon the Macpherson premises because Bowrings, next door, is filled with ammunition, and might explode if it catches fire. "But he said, even if the fire spares them, it'll be almost as bad as if they were burnt out," Len concluded. "Looters have made away with almost everything." Then he glanced over his shoulder toward Water Street and told us he should get back.

Mama grabbed his arm as he turned to go. "Please tell Mr. Winsor we are safe and waiting for him in the park, just as he wished."

After Len left, I tried to picture wild gangs of looters running up and down Water Street, taking anything they pleased. Even my imagination couldn't quite summon the image.

My stomach growled and I told Mama I was hungry. She began to say we'd just have to wait, when Nettie opened one of her cases. Out came a loaf of bread, a cheese wrapped in cheese cloth and a pot of partridgeberry jam. "Last one," she said as she put the jam pot down. "I was saving it for Mr. Winsor's birthday breakfast."

Mama asked Ruby for a jam spoon and butter knife from the silver chest while Nettie cut the bread with the breadknife she'd brought too. I saw her look toward the homeless lady with her little boy nearby. Mama nodded, then asked me to put on my best manners and ask the lady with the little boy if she'd care to join us. Of course, she was more than happy to.

She introduced herself as Mrs. Bertha Ledwell, and her little son is called Georgie. I'm going to stop now to have some bread and cheese and jam —

Oh! A great gang of men is coming into the park,

covered in smoke and soot, some with holes burnt in their jackets, some coughing. Why so many at once? Maybe the fire is out!

Friday, July 8th, Bannerman Park, evening

I can hardly believe how much I am writing today, but I feel I should capture every detail. The sunlight is fading, but we can see the fire now and it glows like a second, more evil sun as it moves ever closer to our house. Even so, I don't think I will be able to see the page beyond another hour, so I will record the terrible events of this evening while there is light. Those men who came into the park were seeking a moment's respite from fighting the fire and they brought with them news of unimaginable horror. Just as I feared, the flankers and burning debris that blow ahead of the main fire are causing smaller fires to break out everywhere, so the conflagration is impossible to control. This is how Scotland Row caught fire, just opposite our beloved Cathedral. The heat was so intense it melted the lead in the stained glass windows and flankers blew inside the Cathedral. The men were helpless to prevent what happened next. Strong stone walls and a stout slate roof did nothing to protect the building from the flames. The Cathedral of Saint John the Baptist, the pride of our city, is now aflame, along with all the earthly goods that trusting citizens placed inside.

Some of the men were crying when they came into the park, tears washing clean tracks down their soot-stained faces. Mr. Ledwell came with them and we listened as he told his wife this sad story. Now everything the Ledwells own is with them in this park, scarcely more than the clothes on their backs and that rather ugly vase.

As tragic stories of destruction and loss were told around the park, Mr. Michael Power began to play his barrel organ in the distance. He chose "Heart of Oak," which is the song of the Royal Navy, well known to everyone here. Many of us raised our voices where we sat to join in the stirring lyrics.

Come, cheer up, my lads, 'tis to glory we steer,
To add something more to this wonderful year;
To honour we call you, as freemen not slaves,
For who are so free as the sons of the waves?

And even more joined in on the chorus:

Heart of oak are our ships, jolly tars are our men,
We always are ready; steady, boys, steady!
We'll fight and we'll conquer again and again.

Like Alfie and I, many sang through all the verses and when the last strains of the song died away, it was plain to see some had taken heart. Even Mrs. Ledwell had more colour in her cheeks.

Mama leaned over and asked her if, perhaps, Sarah and Alfie and I could take little Georgie closer to the barrel organ? Poor Mrs. Ledwell seemed grateful for this suggestion, and I was happy to move around. We had been sitting for hours.

Crossing the park, I noticed Susie Verge sitting with her mother and father and any number of younger brothers and sisters. Our eyes met, she half smiled and looked away quickly. Mrs. Verge noticed me and scowled.

I complain about Mama, but I cannot imagine life with a mother like Susie's. In winter she's an attendant in the women's changing room at the City Hall Skating Rink, which is a very fine establishment. She was the one who caught the girl who was trying to steal a fur muff last winter, a girl about my age. Mrs. Verge held her by the ear while she harangued the poor child, telling her she would burn in Hell for her sins.

The girls who are mean to Susie are mean to me too, which should make us friends, but Susie will not have friends. She is fiercely clever, easily surpassing girls like me who live in houses filled with books and have plenty of time to read them too. Last year she, along with other girls in our year, won prizes for Holy Scriptures, Reading and Recitation, Grammar, French, Arithmetic and Mapping. And she was the only girl to be awarded the General Proficiency prize.

Seeing Susie made me think of school, and I suddenly stopped in my tracks. Sarah asked me what was wrong. "Our school, Sarah, it's upwind from the Cathedral. Do you think — " I was quite unable to finish my horrible thought.

Sarah told Alfie to take little Georgie ahead to see the barrel organ man, then she turned to me with her mouth set. I had never seen her look so grim, and I confess, it frightened me. "Triffie, if our school is burned down, you are not to go making a fuss about it."

My face crumpled like a used hankie. I wanted to be brave, but I couldn't. At least I managed to keep my voice to a whisper while I listed all the buildings that would also burn around our school. "The Bishop's House!" I cried. "How can we have a homeless bishop?" Then I had a truly terrible thought. "What of the orphans! The orphanage is just behind our school." I had a vision of that sturdy brick building in flames, screaming children inside.

Sarah told me not to be so foolish. She was so absolutely sure that the orphans would have been moved long before the fire reached them. Then she added, "It's a blessing this fire began in the afternoon, not the middle of the night. A great many lives will be spared because of that."

Her voice was barely above a whisper, but even so, she looked around to be sure no one was listening before she continued. "Many poor souls around us have lost everything, Triffie. We mustn't fuss over losses that are not even our own." As I tried to stop my mouth from trembling, Sarah put her arm around my shoulder. "Be brave as those Heart of Oak sailors of olden days. Keep up your spirits for Alfie's sake."

Since then I have managed to keep my feelings in check. Now twilight is deepening, though it brings none of the cool relief that usually comes with night. It sounds as if we're on the edge of a mighty battle as roofs and chimneys crash to the ground nearby. The men who came from the Cathedral are rested, and I heard one tell Mr. Ledwell they will regroup at Flavin's Lane, by our fine electric light works and the Terra Nova Bakery, to make a stand there. If they can stop the fire, our house and the east end of the city will be saved. I dare not let myself imagine they might fail.

Saturday, July 9th

So terrible, so terrible, I cannot write of it.

Sunday, July 10th, Scott Street

I feel a little better today, though the problems that face us now can easily bring tears to my eyes. I am that tired, I find myself wishing to sleep at all hours of the day, which is hardly practical, because I no longer have a bed.

I did not think I would sleep on that terrible night

as the fire came closer and closer, consuming all in its path, but I must have dozed off finally because suddenly it was sunrise, and Papa had found us! I flew into his arms, all cares forgotten. His clothes smelled of smoke. Papa hugged me very close while Sarah and Alfie rushed to join me. He held us as if we were all he had in the world. As I soon discovered, that was close to the truth.

Everything is gone. Papa's premises — the shop, the workshops, the wharves — all of it, burnt to ash. Our house, Papa says, is no more than a smoking pit in the ground, all our fine and beautiful things consumed. Only the old stone warehouse on the South Side remains unharmed. We have that, the clothes on our backs and whatever we grabbed as we left our dear, departed house. Our only consolation is that no one was hurt.

A few of Papa's crowd were with him, but the ones who still had homes to return to were gone, taking however many friends they could house with them. The bedraggled band with us in the park were ash smeared, with red-rimmed eyes. Miss Rosy was positively dishevelled, her white blouse, usually spotless, all besmirched with soot and her hair was half fallen out of the neat chignon she always wears. As I watched, she took a comb from her purse. I was quite shocked to see a lady dressing her hair in public, but no one so much as frowned, not even Mama.

Although they had lost the battle to save the store and their livelihoods with it, our brave crowd was still in high spirits, regaling one another with stories of small victories, as if they had defeated the fire. It seemed strange to find them in such good cheer.

The fire had not made its way beyond Rawlins Cross, so the houses around the park were untouched. Soon, neighbours very kindly appeared with food. No one asked them to — they acted out of pure sympathy. Nettie got out the last of our bread and cheese and partridgeberry jam, and we added that to the general store of food that was shared around. No one thought to hold back that morning. There must have been over a thousand people in the park, but we were like one family, bedraggled and dazed, rich and poor alike, together in our misfortune.

Alfie was enthralled by stories of the battle to save Papa's store, but I could not share the good spirits of those around me. I had often thought a sudden reversal of fortune might be romantic, but the grim truth is pure misery. "What is to become of us?" I dared to ask as we finished our meal.

Papa told us that Mr. Sampson had invited us to stay, so we might have a roof over our heads while Papa makes arrangements. Then he said we must be brave for him if we are to recover our fortunes. "The old stone warehouse is not clean, but it's sturdy. I propose we tidy it up and live there for a time."

"Oh, Gregory," Mama cried, "Surely we could find a little cottage to rent!"

Papa shook his head. "It would be very wrong, Eleanor, to do so when we have a place to live, however humble it may be. Thousands are utterly homeless. Besides, I have a plan." Then he said that new stock that was ordered in the spring is already bound for us in ships, and he wants to set up a store as soon as possible. He proposed we have everything under one roof, store and dwelling place, just as his parents had when he was a child.

I saw Mama's face. The one roof Papa grew up under covered a fine brick building on Water Street, not a filthy old warehouse.

I looked around the park at all the homeless people, trying to find a way to feel grateful for our situation, and there was May! She was with her mother, who was handing out buns of bread from a large basket. I asked permission to go to May at once. As I ran to her, I thought of Ordnance House with its many empty rooms. The Seawards, being so charitable, would surely fill their house with homeless families.

May ran to me when I called her and we embraced as if we had not seen each other for months, and it felt that way too. Because the Seawards were on a Mission of Mercy, I had assumed all was well with them, but before one word was said, May's face told another story. I thought of that big, beautiful house and it was like losing Windsor Castle all over again.

"Oh, May! Not Ordnance House!"

She nodded, too overcome to speak. Finally she said in a small voice, "The fire stopped just the other side of the ordnance yard. The trees in Cavendish Square are still quite as green as ever."

Cavendish Square is a small strip of land between the railway station and the ordnance yard, just beyond her home. It was too cruel. May took heart as she spoke, adding that it's lucky the railway station is unharmed. She said the telegraph office had been destroyed, but the telegraphers were already on the go in the railway station, sending out a notice of distress. "Soon, the world will come to our rescue," she concluded. "The bishop said so himself at breakfast."

Breakfast with the bishop? That made me ask where May was staying.

"At Avalon Cottage, near the theology college on Forest Road. It belongs to the church. Our family and the bishop's family, and all the bachelor clerics who lived in the clergy house beside the orphanage, all of us are there, along with all our servants, of course."

I said it sounded crowded, and she admitted it was, but there were plans to send all the theology students who live in the house out around the island for the summer to make more room. "The bishop will return to England on the first possible crossing," May added, "so he can begin to raise money to rebuild the Cathedral."

My heart leapt up. "He thinks it may be restored?"

"He is quite determined."

It was the best news I'd heard since the fire. Then I told May of Papa's plans.

"Your father is a clever man, Triffie, but I will miss having you close by — "

"And our walks to school," I added. "To think the school is gone — "

"And Ashton Cottage, Triffie. It burned too. Now you will never live there."

May and I began to cry, right there in the park, and we sank to the ground with our arms around each other while we recited a litany of all the places we would never see again. The Athenaeum! The City Hall Skating Rink! The Customs House! The Total Abstinence Hall, the British Hall and the Old Factory! All the theatres where we had seen such lovely entertainments.

It was a shameful display, but we couldn't stop ourselves. We were not the only ones crying in the park that morning, though we were soon the loudest. May's mother had wandered far afield with her basket. My mother was closer, so she found us.

"Triffie! May!" She stood over us with her hands on her hips. But we must have looked wonderful sad, because her frown softened a little and so did her voice as she knelt to tell us that we must be brave, for at least we were all unharmed. "Mr. Ledwell said that a man and his six children died in the fire," she told us as she handed us each a hankie and bid us dry our eyes. Then she began to question May about her circumstances. Mama is good at cheering people up when she puts her mind to it and May was quite herself by the time Mrs. Seaward came to collect her.

Papa told us to watch for Mr. Morrissey. One of our tailors who lives out Quidi Vidi way had promised to ask Mr. Morrissey to fetch us "as soon as it seemed decent to call in on him." Until Papa said that, I hadn't realized how very early it was. At this time of year, the sun rises near 5 a.m. Alfie spotted Mr. Morrissey first, and I was disappointed to find he had come with a plain cart, not his usual cab. The wagon was big enough to hold all of us, and even Mama's barrel of good china, but I had been looking forward to seeing one thing from my past that had not been consumed.

Papa directed him to take a roundabout route, over to Merrymeeting through Georgestown so we would not breathe the smoke still rising from the ruins. Passing those comfortable wooden homes from the back of a wooden wagon brought me to realize how much everything would now change. Papa had always sent Mr. Morrissey's fine Victoria cab, with its pretty leather hood, to bring Sarah and me home from school in foul weather. I recalled how I'd often bribed Mr. Morrissey to bring May too, with the promise of some of Nettie's gingerbread. The cabmen in our city pride themselves on their singing, and Mr. Morrissey has a fine voice indeed. May especially likes shipwreck ballads, even if they end with everyone dead, and I remembered all the times she'd sat with me in the Victoria cab with tears streaming down her cheeks, only to ask him to sing another sad ballad when the song ended.

I thought about the songs I like best, the funny ones that Mr. Johnny Burke writes. I bought them from the newsboys for a penny a sheet. Now there would be no school to come home from, no streets of shops to walk along, perhaps no newspapers or song sheets for the newsboys to sell. The little, happy things I took for granted, never dreaming they could be lost — now gone, all gone.

As I tried to hold back my tears, I wished Mr. Morrissey might favour us with one of Johnny Burke's funny songs, but he was so silent and cheerless as he drove, anyone would think he had been burnt out himself. I struggled alone to hide my feelings rather than make everyone even sadder, until we reached the Sampson house here on Scott Street, at the very outskirts of town.

Writing this account has drained me. I need to curl up for a nap somewhere.

Monday, July 11th, Scott Street

I am writing very, very carefully as I sit here at Mrs. Sampson's sewing table in my rose satin dress, once the best of many, now one of two. If I stain it with ink, I will cry. We will leave Scott Street in a few hours, and I am very sorry, though it's clear we cannot stay. The Sampson boys have been sleeping on the parlour rug with Alfie since we came. Mama sleeps in little William's bed, and Sarah and I are squashed into Charles's. Nettie and Ruby sleep in a glassed-in porch on wicker furniture! This house is small and Mr. Sampson's snores almost shake the walls.

I've missed Papa, for he has been working night and day to make the old warehouse fit for us. We have disrupted the Sampsons' lives completely even though we've tried to be helpful. Nettie and Ruby took over the kitchen and Sarah and I look after the boys.

Mrs. Sampson is very clever with her sewing machine and much in demand. Mama told Mrs. Sampson she hoped our help would free her to devote herself to dressmaking, but the poor lady is quite undone by Mama's presence. It's a sin. She hardly seems to know whether to sit or stand when we are alone, and those moments are rare, as neighbour women keep dropping by to hear our story and gossip about the fire. Some of their tales are alarming and no one can agree on the number of people who died. That man with his six children is still spoken of as fact. Three children are missing and presumed drowned, though no one can say how or why, and some say a woman, her daughter and their servant died on Victoria Street. When the neighbour women aren't talking about death and dying, they gossip about all the looting that went on while the fire raged, some whispering darkly they can never tell what they know. The Sampsons have done their very best, but this place is hardly a refuge for us.

I realized how frayed our nerves are when Sarah and I talked this morning, while the boys played in a vacant field near the house, running and yelling in spite of the heat, which is as bad as ever. Though the sun was hot, I was glad to put my company manners aside. I told Sarah I'd never realized that staying in someone else's home could be such a trial.

"It's time for us to be gone, Triffie. The house is bursting at the seams. Mrs. Sampson will have the vapours if we stay, she is that rattled by Mama's presence, and those nosy neighbour women give us no peace."

"Why doesn't Mama just shoo them out of the house and tell Mrs. Sampson to sit down?" I asked.

Sarah looked shocked. "Triffie, think of your manners! A lady cannot ever take command of another lady's home."

"Not even if it's for her own good?"

Sarah shook her head. "Mama is the guest. Only the hostess may take the lead, do you see?"

I frowned. "I can't ever picture myself as a lady, Sarah. So many rules!"

Sarah said she couldn't see how I would ever make my way in the world if I didn't at least try to learn the rules. Her tone was sharp enough to sting, so I told her I had no intention of making my way in the world for quite some time to come, thank you very much. This seemed to make her furious and I could see we were winding up for a real set-to. Thankfully, Alfie called because William was stuck in an apple tree.

At noon we were delighted to find that Papa had come with Mr. Sampson, and Nettie laid out a fine cold dinner with lettuce and egg salad sandwiches. Food is scarce with so many shops burnt out, but Mrs. Sampson keeps her own garden and a few chickens and Nettie is clever, so we have been eating well. Papa had bought some cod from fishermen who live in Fort Amherst at the mouth of the Narrows on the South Side, and everyone was delighted by the prospect of fresh fish for supper. Mrs. Sampson is less nervous when her husband is home. Mr. Sampson holds himself to be equal to anyone (as well he might) and the neighbour women scatter when he appears.

While we ate, Papa told us Mr. Morrissey would be by this evening to move us to our new home. Papa warned that the burnt-out city will be a great shock, and we must prepare to be brave. I confess, living here, it has been easy to put thoughts of the devastation from my mind. The few times Alfie suggested we walk toward the harbour, I quickly dissuaded —

Later

Mama made me stop writing so Sarah and I could pack our belongings and look around to be sure we aren't leaving anything behind. After supper, we'll be ready to go. I feel a little bit sick with apprehension. Sarah, however, is greatly relieved because of what happened earlier. I should have known there was something wrong when she snapped at me. This is what happened.

When dinner was over, Mama said we should take stock before we moved, to see what we'd rescued from the fire and find out what we now own. After Nettie and Ruby tidied the kitchen, we sat in the Sampsons' back garden. Mama asked who wanted to go first, and I volunteered.

I had my writing desk and my journal, of course, and all my sketching books. Mama smiled, for at least we have pen and ink and paper. Papa was pleased (and Alfie was delighted) to find I'd rescued the good brass spyglass, which they'd both thought lost. I had also brought my copies of *Grimms' Fairy Tales* and *Alice's Adventures in Wonderland* (which I dearly love) and *A Child's Garden of Verses*. I had my Fancy Needlework piece too, though no one will be impressed by it now, with the embroidery silks and my needle case, my jewel box and the coin bank Mr. Matt had made for me in the shape of the Customs House.

Papa asked if there was money in my bank, and I shook it so he could hear the coins I've been saving for treats on Regatta Day. But I was most proud because I had packed some clothing — my rose satin dress with a pink sash. It's brand new and I was saving it for Regatta Day too.

I expected Mama to be pleased but she laughed when she saw it. "Oh my, this will be out of place in our new home." My face must have fallen, because she patted my hand. "Never mind, dear. It will serve for Sundays." Then she told me I could soon put it on so Nettie could launder my everyday dress and pinafore, which, she said, would dry in no time in this weather. She wants us to leave here in clean clothes.

Alfie came next. He'd packed his bag of marbles, all his tin soldiers and his brand new copies of *Treasure Island* and *Kidnapped,* which we haven't even read yet. He also had a spare sailor suit and stockings, and his Sunday shoes. So Alfie turned out to be more practical than I am.

Even so, Mama declared she had no inkling she'd raised such impractical children. Everything that happened on the day of the fire is etched on my memory, so I recall exactly what Mama told us when she sent us up that beautiful mahogany staircase one last time. "You said we should take whatever we valued most, and that's what we did."

My excellent memory didn't seem to please Mama at all. She replied that she felt sure she could depend on Sarah to be more sensible, and of course she was right. Sarah's valise was filled with her collection of hat trimmings — velvet and satin ribbons and flowers and feathers, but underneath, it was plain her clothing filled much of the space. I expected Sarah might gloat a little, but she did the most amazing thing instead. Her hands flew up to her face and she burst into tears!

"My dear, whatever is wrong?" Mama asked as Papa pressed a clean hankie into Sarah's hand.

Tears continued to stream down her face as she spoke. She told us she had always felt quite certain a sad reversal of fortune would force her to earn a living. She sniffed and raised her chin and said she was happy because she had feared we would be orphaned when that day arrived, and at least no one had died. (She looked anything but happy while she said this.) Then she told us she was packed and perfectly prepared to go to Halifax and seek employment as a milliner's assistant, sending as much of her earnings home as she could to help recover our fortunes.

I always knew those novels she spent so much time

reading were not an Improving Influence, but she looked so very miserable, I couldn't say so.

Papa and Mama both assured Sarah they would never let her do such a thing. Then Papa explained that, unlike most people, we are not without means. In time, there will be insurance money for the house and the store, and he reminded Sarah of the candy money. Winsor's penny candy and boiled sweets are shipped all across the island, and the money that is owed on account will trickle in for months to come. Luckily, Papa told us, the summer candy was shipped weeks ago, and that will provide a source of income.

Little by little, Sarah brightened as she realized her life was not to be ruined after all and Mama coaxed her to show us what else she had managed to save. Tucked into the pocket of her valise, where they would not crush the trimmings, were her copies of *Jane Eyre* and *Wuthering Heights*, and she opened her jewel box to show me her strands of coral and pearls, and the amethyst brooch which belonged to Nanny Winsor. I have always coveted that brooch so I was glad to see it safe.

Then it was Mama's turn, and she confessed that she was hardly more practical than Alfie or me. She has been so intent on saving the china and silver, she'd only saved a few clothes for her and Papa and her best jewels. "What good will fine china and silver do us in our new home?" she added. "The under-clothes I wrapped the dishes in will be more useful."

Then she turned to Nettie. "I imagine you've saved us from ourselves, haven't you? What are you hiding in those valises?"

Out came five sharp kitchen knives, a sturdy tea-pot, a kettle, a small frying pan, a tin ladle, a mixing bowl, a tea tray, a small bag of flour and packets of tea, salt and sugar, yeast and bread soda, all wrapped in clean tea towels.

Mama thanked Nettie, saying that would make a good start on a new kitchen for us. Then Alfie asked what she had in the unopened case.

"Every stitch I owns," Nettie replied. "And there's no need to be putting my corsets on display for ye." We all laughed and Alfie blushed.

Now all eyes went to Ruby, who of course had packed her clothes. She reminded us she'd also car-ried the silver chest, then she looked directly at Papa. "I saved just about every penny you ever paid me, Mr. Winsor. The bank notes is sewed into the hem of my skirt. So, if you needs it to tide you over 'till the candy money comes in, I can lend it back to you."

This was so bold, I wondered if Papa would think she was being cheeky, but he replied as if she were an adult, telling Ruby she was kind to offer, but it wouldn't be necessary.

Then Papa made a speech, as he is fond of doing

on special occasions, at home and at work as well. Mama always tells us we must listen and remember, because Papa thinks carefully about what he wants to say, and he is wise. He rose to his feet and said we must put the fire behind us. What's lost is lost, and no good would come of dwelling on the past. We can only move on by looking ahead to a brighter future.

When he finished, Mama shooed us back into the house and I changed into this lovely dress. This entry is almost finished and I'm happy to report the dress is not stained and Sarah is more like herself than she has been since the fire.

Wednesday, July 13th, South Side Warehouse

We are so busy arranging our new dwelling, I have little time to write. Even if I did, it's hard to think because of all the noise. Hammers echo across the harbour from sunrise to sunset as people build shelters, and even start new homes. Nettie says it sounds like an army of woodpeckers. If that weren't enough, the Royal Marines from the HMS *Emerald* are blasting down brick walls along Water and Duckworth Streets. Sudden booms sweep across the harbour to rattle the windows and make us all jump. Papa says they must do this because the walls are unsafe. One of his competitors spent two days building a temporary shed inside the ruins of their old store so they could resume business, only to have a wall collapse on it, destroying everything. If it hadn't happened at night, someone might have been killed.

At least we have this sound, if dusty, building to put a roof over our heads, and for that we must be grateful.

Papa goes to the ruin of his store almost every day to see how the cleanup is coming along, and he tells us most of his crowd now have shelter too, even if it's just a corner in someone's house to curl up in. A few have made the best of the situation. Mr. McAllister, the canny old bachelor, has taken a long-planned holiday to visit his sister in Scotland, which is wise because we have no need of inside workers now.

Papa can only employ some of his men to clear away the rubble from the store site. Mr. Stabb is supervising and Mr. Sampson will join him now that the warehouse is livable. I asked Papa when we would begin to rebuild, but he says that can't happen until the new street lines are settled. Many people want Water Street to be wider to prevent fires in the future, but no one wants to lose land. Mama worries about the ladies. We will have no work for them until new stock arrives and we set up shop here, and that may take weeks.

Our new neighbours are very kind. They keep dropping in with small gifts of household goods for us, some quite old and used, but all given with good heart.

I must go for Mama is calling. She is very downcast by our situation here, I'm afraid, so I am trying to be extra good and helpful.

Friday, July 15th, South Side Warehouse

One week ago today, Alfie got stuck in the dumb waiter, and it seemed like the worst thing that ever happened. Now, every time I think things can get no worse, we slip even deeper into the abyss of despair. But I should tell the story in the proper order.

By the time Mr. Morrissey arrived, I was back in my everyday dress with a good fish supper inside me, feeling much refreshed. He'd brought his cart again, with all the things rescued from the store as the fire closed in when Miss Rosy was so brave. Our cabman helped Mr. Sampson lift the china barrel, then Papa made another little speech to thank the Sampsons for taking us in, and shook Mr. Sampson's hand. Papa and Mama squeezed together with Mr. Morrissey on the driver's seat, while Nettie, Sarah, Alfie, Ruby and I settled into the cart. We said our goodbyes as if we were setting out on a long journey, and Mrs. Sampson tried to look regretful at our going.

As we drove toward the harbour along Freshwater Road, Mr. Morrissey was once again silent and out of sorts. This time Mama noticed, and she asked if he were quite well (which is a polite way of saying "are you ailing?"). He replied that he was feeling out of sorts because, "It's a sad thing to discover your neighbours are nothing more than common thieves."

When Mama protested that he must be wrong, Mr. Morrissey launched into a rant about "all the sleeveens in Quidi Vidi Village with fine Persian rugs on their floors, and chicken coops stuffed to the gills with fine china and silver." He concluded with, "And just try telling those fellas they are in the wrong!"

We were so shocked, the horse clopped along in silence for a good few minutes. Finally Mama told him, if people around him had failed to live up to his standards of honesty, it only served to show what a gentleman he is. To call someone a gentleman is the very highest honour Mama can bestow, and, although he said nothing, I think Mr. Morrissey knew as much.

To save our cab man further embarrassment, Mama changed the subject, asking Papa where we would fetch our water from, and I listened closely as Papa began to talk about our new neighbours. He told us there was a cooperage across the street, run by a man named Mr. Critch, and that the Critches have offered us use of the well in their garden.

"Oh me nerves," Nettie said when she heard this, "back to hauling water. I knew them pipes was too good to be true." Then she looked at Ruby. "Put some muscle on you, hauling those pails will."

Papa laughed and said that wouldn't be necessary, because he could haul the water himself, or Mr. Matthew Bright would. This surprised everyone. Papa even managed to surprise himself.

"I can't believe I forgot to tell you!" he said. "Matthew's boarding house is gone, of course. He spent one night in the old drill shed, and it wasn't to his liking. I have no need of him at present, but there's plenty of work for tinsmiths." Papa explained that many stoves survived the fire, but the stovepipes did not. Mr. Matt has hired on with a tinsmith in the west end, making and fitting stovepipes. When he learned that Papa was living in the stone warehouse, Mr. Matt asked if we would give him a corner for his bed, and Papa was happy to. "In return," Papa continued, "he will share whatever he earns. These are strange times and he is paid in kind as often as cash. I've hardly seen him since he arrived. He's up at first light and not back until dark. It's easy to forget he's there."

The idea of having Mr. Matt so close was cheering, but as Papa spoke we reached the top of the hill and I gasped before I could stop myself. Below us spread the charred remains of our beloved city. The walls of our Cathedral still stood, and the Methodist church before it, both now burnt-out shells. Around them, chimneys rose like a forest of blasted trees. We saw all this through a haze of smoke. The day was hot, but I suddenly felt hotter still and very thirsty.

Alfie asked Papa where all the smoke was coming from. The fire had been out for almost three days. Papa explained that coal is still burning in basements. Even when that burns out, the coal depots may burn for weeks. Papa said no one knows how to put those fires out but at least there's nothing left around them to catch fire.

As Mr. Morrissey guided his horses down Long's Hill into the very heart of destruction, the suffocating smell of burnt wood and lime and coal smoke grew ever stronger. Alfie began to wheeze and Sarah found a clean hankie so he might cover his nose.

Mama soon asked Mr. Morrissey if he could take us away from the dreadful smoke. Alfie was finding it hard to catch his breath. He apologized, explaining that the gentle slope of Long's Hill was easier on the horses. As we turned onto Queen's Road, my eyes were drawn, with a kind of horrid fascination, to the naked chimneys that were the only remains of the lovely Synod Hall where Sarah and I had gone to school. Thankfully, the cart now moved away from the blackened remnants of the fire and soon everyone found it easier to breathe.

When we came to the Long Bridge, I kept my eyes to the right, on the peaceful triangle of water at the end of the harbour where everything is green and quiet and quite untouched by the fire, only reluctantly looking ahead to our new neighbourhood, the

South Side. It hardly looks like the St. John's I know, stretching along a narrow strip of land, wedged between the harbour and South Side hills, which loom toward the sky. If you didn't look back, you could easily take it to be a bustling little outport with an astonishing amount of industry. Whitewashed warehouses and cooperages crowd the waterfront so thickly that the road behind them disappears. Where wharves and fish flakes cover the shoreline, we could see women and children gathering yaffles of split and salted cod to stow away from the evening damp.

At the end of the Long Bridge, we faced St. Mary's parish hall. It's a sturdy, plain building and I suddenly wondered if I would go to school there in the fall. We turned onto the South Side Road, passing the fine old stone rectory and St. Mary's church, our church now. On the right, climbing up the hills, there were a few rows of frame houses, some neatly kept, some not, and there were even some old stone houses. Fenced meadows that seemed to be mostly rock reached up the steep hill toward wild barrens.

The smell of fish was overwhelming. On the harbour side, among the wharves and warehouses, I saw the oil pots where cod livers sat brewing into cod liver oil. Sarah, Alfie and I held our noises, but Ruby did not. Nettie said, "That's an honest stink, that is. Our nation is built upon that smell, my duckies. Never forget that."

Papa asked Mr. Morrissey to halt the cart and pointed out the warehouse that is now our home, a solidly-made building of whitewashed stone. There are three storeys from ground to attic. The bottom floor is without windows. The second floor is lined with little windows and the attic sits under a peaked roof that sports a few dormers. Outside, it looked quite cheerful, but as we entered, I realized it was not a home. The ground level is a vast, dark, open space with a dirt floor, filled with empty wooden crates. "This is for storage," Papa said. "It is not clean and there are mice. The wooden crates have proven useful though, as you'll soon see."

I confess that the gloom frightened me and I went up the stairs as fast as I could. There are no risers, so you can see through as you go up, which made me a bit dizzy. The second floor is much brighter, with its many small windows on either side, and there's a wooden floor, though it's rough and bare. Papa told us we will make our shop there as he led us up another flight of stairs to our new home. The long attic walls slope at the pitch of the roof. The only light comes from windows on the straight walls at either end, and three dormer windows on either side set into the sloping walls a good distance apart. On the harbour side of the building, by the windows, Papa has made a living space for us. Mr. Matt lives at the other end behind a wall made from old crates. The space is mostly open, but we have small dressing closets, also made of crates, so at least we have privacy to change.

I am too tired and discouraged to continue my story, and the light fades quickly in this hovel, so I will put away my writing for today.

Saturday, July 16th, South Side Warehouse

I don't think I fully understood how humble our circumstances had become until we arrived here. Our beds are straw pallets on boards laid across old crates. We have no blankets as yet, but the heat is stifling so we do not need them. When we arrived, Papa proudly showed us the chairs he and Mr. Sampson made by cutting down empty barrels they found in the warehouse. They are very rough indeed and we must watch for snags and slivers. We have only an old fish-splitting table where food can be prepared, and no table for eating. I am very lucky to have my little travel desk to write on.

Until Papa is able to salvage the stove from the ruins of our house, we have no way to cook food, so our meals are cold. This is not the hardship it would be in winter, but many of the cold foods Nettie would like to prepare for us — potato salad, for example — require a stove. Yesterday a man came around selling milk and hard-boiled eggs, and that was a treat. Even bread is hard to find because so many bakeries burned and, of course, Nettie has no way to bake. A ham sandwich has become something of a rare delicacy. Wednesday night we dined on cheese and ham alone. Nettie cannot even boil water for tea because we dare not light an open fire on the patch of land beside the wharf. The hot, dry weather has not changed and everything is still dry as tinder.

I am trying to be brave, but we are *paupers.* The first night we slept here, something woke me. When I listened, I could hear Mama crying in her bed, very quietly. Mama *never* cries. I am trying hard not to be downcast, but Alfie is still wheezing. Papa has asked Dr. Roberts to come and listen to his chest.

Sunday, July 17th, South Side Warehouse

Alfie is leaving! This is all Ruby's fault. She is a hateful girl and I wish NEVER to see her again. Nettie says I am a cod of misery today, and that's exactly how I feel. Everyone went off to Sunday service at St. Mary's, leaving me here. This was the only punishment Mama could think of, as the fire took care of everything she might once have taken from me. Before they left, Mama sternly commanded me to write in my journal to help me regain my composure. How can I live without Alfie? Everything is terrible, everything is bad and wrong. I hate this journal. I will *not* write today.

Later

I feel a little better now. After I put my journal down, I made such a racket weeping, I drove Mr. Matt from his bed. He works so hard, he was too tired to get up for Sunday service.

"Is someone after being murdered? Did thieves break in to take your mother's silver?" he said when he found me. Even through my tears, I could see the dark smudges under his eyes, and I was ashamed to have disturbed his one day of rest. I sat up and straightened my pinafore and made an effort to calm myself, but I had cried so much, I began to hiccup.

Mr. Matt brought me a cup of water and I told him the whole story. Alfie's breathing troubles began when Mr. Morrissey drove us here, and they have only become worse since. There are still forest fires outside the city and a pall of smoke hangs over everything. The wind blows smoke from smouldering coal heaps right across the harbour, so we can't open the windows, and this hot, close warehouse itself seems to hold the dust of centuries, in spite of Papa's best efforts. Nettie says she's afraid to give the place a good cleaning, because she'll only raise more dust.

Alfie's wheezing fills our ears all night, and he can only sleep on one side. Yesterday Dr. Roberts came across to see him. After listening to Alfie's lungs with his stethoscope, he looked very grave indeed. He took

Mama and Papa aside and they spoke together for a long time.

When he was gone, Mama called us together and told us Dr. Roberts says that Alfie cannot remain here.

Sarah asked if the Sampsons might agree to take him back. It seemed a sensible solution, but Mama shook her head and said we need to remove him from the city altogether, somehow. She turned to Alfie. "You must be very brave, Alfred."

I wondered if I could go with Alfie, to keep him company. I've never been away from my family, but I knew I could be brave if Alfie needed me. That was when Ruby spoke. "I could take Master Alfie to Scilly Cove with me," she said. "You don't really have need of me now that — " She paused to find the right words and Nettie agreed, saying now that there's no proper house to keep, we have no use for two servants.

Ruby went on about how her mother would be happy to have her back with the garden on the go and how wonderful the air would be in Scilly Cove. She'd even worked out Alfie's sleeping arrangement before she was finished.

"The trains are still running," Papa said. "It's lucky the tracks lie beyond the destruction." To my horror, I saw he was taking Ruby's suggestion to heart.

But Mama reminded him that the trains pass right through forest fires, and she told him a story we'd heard at Mrs. Sampson's from a neighbour woman whose brother works as a brakeman. He was on the first train out after the fire, and they had to keep halting the train because of forest fires. It was supposed to reach Harbour Grace in the afternoon, and didn't arrive until 1:30 the following morning, everyone covered in smoke and soot. "It might be even more dangerous for Alfie to travel by train," she concluded.

For a moment, I thought Alfie would stay, then Ruby spoke again. "There's almost always a schooner or two from somewhere near to home in the harbour. I feels certain I'd be able to find us passage on a vessel. I got the cash to pay if need be." She was bound and determined to get home. Papa told Ruby there was no need for her to use her money and, if her parents would agree to take Alfie, his room and board would be equal to her pay.

At that point, Mr. Matt interrupted me to ask whether my parents would let Alfie go off to the house of strangers.

I replied that they would. "Ruby's parents are pillars of the church in Scilly Cove. She came to us with a letter from her clergyman. Mama and Papa feel certain their home is a good one."

As I explained to Mr. Matt, they are going to take Ruby around the harbour later today so she can find an outbound ship, and then send a telegram to her parents. As for Alfie, he is so delighted by the adventure, he has no thought for anything else, least of all what his absence will mean to me.

By the time I finished my story, I was almost in tears again. Mr. Matt sat in one of Papa's barrel chairs, looking solemn. "Well now, Miss Triff," he said at last, "I always took you to be a plucky maid."

"I am full of pluck!" I replied. "I am as brave as a pirate queen! But not without Alfie. And Ruby is such a villain! It's her ambition to get home at any cost."

"Ruby'd be not much older than yourself, is that right?"

I sniffed. "She is a full year older, twelve."

He told me he was "a big lad of eighteen" when he left his family to come work in town, and thought he "would die of the homesickness" his first year, even though he went home for Christmas. Then he asked whether Ruby had been home since she came to town.

I conceded that she had not.

"Put yourself in her shoes for a moment," Mr. Matt said. "She sees a chance to get her heart's desire and do some good at the same time. Does that sound like a villain to you?"

I knew what he wanted me to say, I knew what I should say, but I could not. "It does from where I stand," I told him.

He stood and gave me a pat on the head. "Then you must try to stand in a better light, my duckie."

When I saw that even a kind and fair man like Mr. Matt would not take my side, I knew my cause was lost. He went to draw a pail of water, and I took up my journal again to write all this down. Without Alfie, my heart will be well and truly broken. I will not cry, I will not argue. But when Alfie goes, I will take to my hard, comfortless bed and there I will remain.

Wednesday, July 20th, South Side Warehouse

Sweet rain is dripping off the roof eaves, which sit just below our floor here in the attic, and pattering merrily against the windows, washing away the soot from the fire. We are pleased to find the roof is sound, with no leaks. With the help of his pocket knife, Papa forced a few of the windows open and, for the first time, cool, fresh air sweeps through the warehouse.

When I think back over the past few days, I burn with shame. Mama and Papa took Ruby around the harbour on Sunday afternoon, but they couldn't find a schooner headed for Trinity Bay South. Even so, this gave me no hope, I was that worried about losing Alfie.

Mama had met Mrs. Critch at church, and we were all invited to Sunday supper at the Critch house. It was kind of them to put on an evening meal for us, as Sunday dinner is usually eaten at noon, and a grand meal it was, with salt beef and cabbage and pease pudding. The Critch dining room almost burst at the seams to accommodate us and was as hot as a furnace, but it was the first real meal we'd eaten since we left the Sampsons'. I couldn't enjoy it though, for misery ruined my appetite. Alfie could talk of nothing but sailing to Scilly Cove, and I would talk of nothing at all. In the general hubbub, my silence went unremarked.

On Monday, Papa put the word out among his men, and Mr. Stabb soon found a schooner, the *Yarrow*, out of Heart's Content, that was just about to sail home. There were even a few men from Scilly Cove in the crew, so they were already planning to put in there along the way. They had come to town with a load of lumber for relief and would take no money for Ruby and Alfie's passage, they were that eager to help victims of the fire. Everything was arranged so quickly, I had no time to make peace with it.

I did not say goodbye to Alfie. I pretended to be busy in a corner of the second floor, sweeping, when he left. Mama did not call attention to me and, in his excitement, Alfie failed to notice. As they walked down the stairs, he took Ruby's hand in the most trusting manner. I felt as if some evil magic had transformed her into his sister, and I was now the maid, humble and ignored.

Two men from the *Yarrow* rowed over to our wharf as I watched though a window, my vision blurred as much by tears as the soot on the glass. When Alfie got into the boat beside Ruby, he asked

Mama a question, then looked up at the windows. I was sure he could not see me, but I ducked back anyway, hot tears on my face. It was all I could do to keep from rushing outside to pluck him from the boat. Instead, I forced myself upstairs and lay down on my bed, face to the wall, wishing I had a blanket to pull over my head, though it was far too hot to do any such thing. I knew I would have to keep very still because the boards under the straw pallet do not hold together, and I would have to get up to rearrange the bed if I fidgeted, or fall to the floor. I have no talent for holding still.

Mama said nothing when she saw me on my bed. I understood that she was angry with me for behaving so badly. I could not simply get up and join everyone without suffering a loss of dignity. I was stuck.

I spent the day lying rigid on my bed. At suppertime I saw no reason to get up to eat, especially as no one had been able to locate bread that day. When the meal was finished, Papa suggested it would be a good evening for a stroll, as the wind was blowing in off the sea. He was trying to divert Mama's attention away from me, and I was grateful. Mama asked me, once, if I would come. I could not reply, my throat was that stopped with the tears I could not cry.

Nettie said there was a bakery on Duckworth Street that had narrowly escaped the fire, and she would buy bread from it tomorrow if she had to get up at dawn. Papa told her he would see about our stove this week, their voices fading as they went downstairs.

I think I might have died of grief, or maybe hunger, if Mr. Matt had not returned with a loaf of bread and half a roast chicken, given to him as pay for his day's labour. He went directly for the breadknife on Nettie's old splitting table and gave me no time to be dignified. "Triffie my maid, who could say no to a roast chicken sandwich? The wind's shifted round, and I think we're finally in for a change of weather. Let's eat outside."

The Critches have a bench under the apple tree near their well. Mr. Critch waved to us from the door of his cooperage as Mr. Matt led me into the garden. The burnt-out city is hidden by our warehouse home, and the wind blew down the South Side hills, fresh from the sea. But for the ache in my heart, I could imagine the fire had never happened. I was too sad to talk at first, and Mr. Matt seemed to understand. As we ate, though, I began to wonder where he got this food.

"These people got family that's not burnt out," Mr. Matt explained. "One lady's mother made the bread and another has a sister who keeps chickens over by Patrick Street."

"We used to live on Patrick Street, before Windsor Castle," I told him.

He almost choked on his sandwich. I had to slap

him on the back. When he could talk again, he said he never knew that our family knows what most people called our house.

"I'm the only one," I said and I told him how I found out. By the time we finished our meal, I felt better, though I still ached for Alfie. But I so was tired from being sad, and from the effort to keep still, I crawled into bed and immediately fell asleep. I didn't even hear my family return.

It was dark when I awoke, and Papa had bundled me into his arms. "Come, Tryphena, woebegone creature that you are." I didn't know why he was carrying me downstairs, but he was smiling and something in my heart melted. Everyone else was already on the wharf, staring at the sky, enraptured, when Papa put me down. No lamps shine where the city used to be, so there was no light to hide the beauty above us. Shimmering curtains of green and pink played across the sky, reflected in the black water of the harbour, outshining any fireworks — the aurora borealis.

No one could ever remember seeing the northern lights over St. John's as we saw them last night. We sat on the wharf for a long time, watching, and our neighbours joined us, everyone speechless. Papa sat with his arm around me and Sarah took my hand.

Finally Mama spoke. "It seems the heavens are trying to remind us that life is beautiful, whatever misery besets us," she said. "Triffie, you are not the only one who misses Alfie, and I would very much appreciate a hug."

Sunday, July 24th, South Side Warehouse

Yesterday Nettie remarked that Alfie was "our salt and pepper." Without him, life has no flavour. I am finding it hard to fill my time and I do wish Alfie had left me one of his new books. Mama and Papa are wrapped up in the insurance claims for the house and the store, an endlessly complicated process that leaves them both right crooked and inclined to snap if I ask for anything. Sunday is especially hard. We never work on Sundays. Nettie even peels all the vegetables for Sunday supper on Saturday evening and puts them in a pot of water. The question of how to occupy Sunday afternoons looms large without Alfie and I was glad when Sarah proposed that we write to him. I tore some pages from the back of this book and letter writing took up a good hour or more.

Afterward, Sarah very generously offered to lend me one of her books. As she'd already read *Jane Eyre* to me aloud, I accepted *Wuthering Heights*. It could easily be set in Newfoundland as far as weather goes, but all the overwrought emotions make it very heavy going. It certainly paints a grim picture of being swept away by mad desire.

Wednesday, July 27th, South Side Warehouse

What a busy day for Papa! He found our stove and rescued Mouser.

Papa had engaged Mr. Morrissey to take him around town today. His first stop was the post office, where he registered our new address. Now we'll be sure to get the candy money, and of course letters from Alfie, if he writes us. Mama taught him how to make his letters, but he's not very good with a pen yet. Nettie said, even if Alfie does write, I shouldn't be holding my breath. Ruby was always waiting for mail because the postman only goes out in his cart from Heart's Content toward Scilly Cove a few times a week. I can't help hoping, though.

Next Papa had arranged for Mr. Sampson to meet him at the remains of Windsor Castle. As they poked around in the rubble, he saw a sorry looking creature that, he said, appeared to be a cat. He took no notice, but the cat sat and watched until Papa finally realized it was Mouser. He and Mr. Sampson found our stove, covering themselves in soot and ash in the process, and Mr. Sampson confirmed that it was still in working order. Papa's arranged to have it hauled over here tomorrow and Mr. Matt will bring stovepipe home so he can connect it for us. Mama and Papa are debating where to put it. Nettie is so pleased, she says she doesn't care where it goes.

But back to Mouser. Papa knew she would never

sit still for a carriage ride, but he had brought a brin bag in case he found small things in the ruins. Mouser looked half starved, Papa said, and Mr. Sampson had brought along his lunch, a kipper sandwich, so they lured her over and Papa put her in the bag! Then, of course, the carriage had to detour over here to deliver her to us. She howled all the way, and Papa no longer looked respectable in his sooty clothes. People cast such dark glances, Papa was sure they thought he'd been up to mischief.

Mouser was still howling when he carried her in, but as soon as she walked out of the bag and saw us, she stopped. I took some damp brin to her, and instead of scratching me or running away, she sat and purred while I rubbed soot from her fur. Nettie had just managed to buy a bit of butter from a woman who keeps a cow up the South Side Road and she spared a little to rub on Mouser's paws the once. Nettie says, when Mouser licks the butter off her paws, she will catch the scent of her new home and know she belongs here. There are plenty of mice running around this warehouse, so we are as happy to see Mouser as she is to see us.

Other things are settling in too — the coal fires are finally out. Papa said one merchant, at his wit's end, offered half of his land on the harbourfront to anyone who could extinguish his stockpile of anthracite. Mr. Mallard, a very clever merchant of wines, scrounged as many buckets as he could and hired fifty men at a dollar a day. They worked in two lines, one passing buckets full of water to the coal and the other passing empty buckets back to the harbour, pouring water on the coal until it finally went out. It sounds like something out of a fairy tale, but it's true! Sarah is going to put the whole story in the letter we are writing to Alfie. We'll also tell him about Mouser. Without Alfie, she would surely have perished in the fire. I do wish he had been here to see her come out of that brin bag.

Friday, July 29th, South Side Warehouse

Our biggest newspapers, *The Evening Telegram* and *The Evening Herald*, were burnt out in the fire. Only *The Royal Gazette* managed to stay afloat, and one other newspaper, *The Morning Despatch,* started up only the week before last. Because paper is so scarce, both are just a few pages and not many copies are printed, so real news is hard to come by and rumours abound. Last night Mr. Matt came home in time to join us for supper with a copy of *The Morning Despatch*. (He also brought a set of stovepipes, which we all declared to be mostly beautifully made.)

Sarah and I read every scrap of that newspaper today. It seems there was no man lost to the fire along with his six children, as we heard on that first morning in the park. That was just a rumour. Considering the terrible loss of house and home, very few people perished. A Mrs. Stephens who kept a shop on Victoria Street died along with her daughter and their maid, because the invalid daughter was too slow getting out of the house, it seems. This daughter had a child, and a man who boarded with the family had already taken this child to safety. When he returned, he found the house aflame and felt certain everyone must have escaped. With people scattered all over the city, it was days before he realized the terrible fate that had befallen them, and longer still before the ruin was safe enough to discover the bodies. Another woman died in her house on Bulley's Lane, and a few more are said to be missing.

The story of Mrs. Stephens, her invalid daughter and their servant was so affecting, Sarah and I began to cry as we read it. Nettie was over by the windows where the light is better, cutting one of Mama's petticoats up to make curtains. She demanded to know why we were making such a racket, and ended up in tears herself when she read the story.

But the paper also contains much encouraging news about relief that is coming to us from all over the world, just as the bishop told May it would on the morning after the fire. It is heartening to know, for example, that the New York Stock Exchange has taken up "a handsome subscription" for our city, and the soldiers of the Garrison in Halifax willingly gave up a day's pay to help us, a sum of $750! The City of Chicago, of course, is very much interested in our plight, remembering their own Great Fire of 1871, which was much more terrible than ours. It seems cities as far away as Britain, the United States and our neighbours in nearby Canada are moved to come to our aid.

The paper listed some figures compiled by the Relief Committee and I am going to record them here, so I will always remember how truly terrible this fire was. These are the numbers of people made homeless and property destroyed:

No. of Families 1,874
No. of Persons 10,234
No. of Houses (estimated) 1,250

This paper also listed the places where the homeless live now:

Bannerman Park 1,021
Quidi Vidi 124
Parade Rink 136
Near Railway Depot 190
Drill Shed 65

TOTAL 1,536

Most people who were burnt out found some kind of shelter with family or friends or, like us, they had resources to fall back upon. Mama said only fifteen per cent of the people displaced by the fire are truly homeless now. She added it would be terrible if any of Papa's crowd were among them. Papa has assured her that schooners are arriving daily, loaded with lumber for relief, and men are building sheds, digging latrines and putting up clotheslines. Bannerman Park is a shantytown, but Papa says meals and all manner of relief are provided to those who live there. When he said this, I remembered Miss Rosy sitting on the grass the morning after the fire, dressing her hair, and asked if Miss Rosy could be living there. Papa said he believed she might be, and Mama vowed that we will soon go to the park to see. When Papa opens up his shop here, Mama wants to hire those who are most in need first.

Nettie is calling us to supper now.

Friday, July 29th, after supper

Something in *The Morning Despatch* puzzled us very much. While we ate supper tonight, Sarah asked about it and I was glad she did.

"Papa," she said, "on the last page of *The Morning Despatch* that Mr. Matt brought home, there was a summary of the sermon preached in the Roman Catholic Cathedral last Sunday."

"I'm glad, at least, that the Catholics in our crowd still have a cathedral to worship in," Mama said. She went on to say that she wished the paper had included a summary of the sermon given at St. Thomas's for the congregation of our Cathedral last Sunday. Though there's a perfectly good Church of England in our new neighbourhood, she still wishes she could worship with those who share our losses.

Papa patted her hand and reminded her, as he has many times since we moved here, that it is better for us to befriend our new neighbours and show we are happy to be among them.

Sarah persisted, getting to the heart of the matter. She said the priest expressed hope that our Cathedral would soon be restored, but he also spoke of the property that was stolen the day of the fire.

Mama exclaimed that this was very forthright of him.

Sarah had Papa's full attention now. He asked her what she'd read.

Sarah told him what had puzzled us both. The priest had said those who had stolen property that was sitting somewhere already recovered from the fire should return it.

I couldn't contain myself. "He seemed to be saying people could *keep* things that were stolen out of houses in the path of the fire."

Sarah nodded. "That can't be right, can it? We must have misunderstood."

Mr. Matt spoke up. "Law of salvage."

I asked him what that meant.

He said that when a ship is abandoned at sea, it's fair play to take whatever can be rescued from it. Or after a ship is wrecked, anyone who can get goods off can claim ownership of them. He went on to explain that the law of salvage is one reason a captain will stay on a ship at all costs when trouble arises.

"But surely that law doesn't apply on *land*!" Mama had gone quite red.

"No, Mrs. Winsor, it should not. It's complicated enough to apply that law at sea," Mr. Matt said.

But we were left to wonder. If someone stole property from a house that was *about* to burn, *our* house for instance, would it be theirs to keep?

Sunday, July 31st, South Side Warehouse

Today the usual monotony of Sunday afternoon was relieved by a lovely surprise. Just as Sarah and I were finishing our weekly letter to Alfie, someone pounded on the door below. (It's a good distance from our attic to the door, so pounding is required.) Papa went downstairs and returned with May, her mother and Miss Maude Seaward, who had come for a visit. Nettie bustled away to make tea while we settled our visitors on chairs and benches as best we could. The Seaward ladies looked about with kind eyes, paying many compliments to our makeshift arrangements. I could never have imagined that Mama would entertain May's family in an old warehouse, or that everyone would be so pleased.

We learned that the Seaward family are still living in Avalon Cottage on Forest Road. This has been a busy time for them, as all requests for relief must be verified, and clergymen are considered most reliable witnesses, so people come to Avalon Cottage with their relief orders day and night. Church aid is also being arranged for the needy, and that was one reason for this visit. (It shocked me to think anyone would regard our family as part of "the needy.")

Miss Maude told us that the bishop has been busy inspiring sympathy in England and a shipment of clothing will soon arrive from the St. Andrews Waterside Church Mission in London. Then Nettie brought tea, and Mrs. Seaward exclaimed as she took the cup, "Oh, is this your wedding china?"

Mama averred that it was indeed.

"So lovely," Mrs. Seaward said, caressing the saucer. "I fear we rescued nothing of value. So many treasures lost." She asked if we had heard rumours of all the houses that had been looted the night of the fire and Mama said yes, we had.

"We have faint hope that anything was taken from Ordnance House," May's mother continued, "as the doors were stout and firmly locked."

Mama laughed and said that our door stood wide open the night of the fire.

Mouser was resting nearby and it was too much for me to resist. The whole story came pouring out of me, starting with the china barrel, ending with Papa's discovery of Mouser. By the time I finished, the Seawards looked quite astonished.

Mama regained control of the conversation with a meaningful look. "We were lucky enough to recover Mouser. It seems incredible to hope our property might be returned. We have accepted our losses."

"Yes," Mrs. Seaward replied. "And you are so lucky to live under your own roof."

I looked around our vast warehouse, filled with odds and ends of furniture and stacked crates, and realized she was right. When I first came here, I thought it a hovel, but I'm starting to feel at home.

As May and I had now spent a polite interval behaving (or, in my case, almost behaving) I wondered if I could be allowed to show her our new neighbourhood. I wasn't sure the Seaward ladies would agree, but they did, and we hurried off before they could change their minds. I showed May where we will make our shop, and we went outside to Mrs. Critch's garden, where the scent of flowers almost overpowers the smell of fish.

May told me that our school is going to reopen in the fall.

"But how can it?" I asked her, since all the buildings around the Cathedral are gone.

May knew everything because the school board meets at Avalon Cottage and Miss Cowling often comes to discuss details. "There's an old schoolhouse beside St. Thomas's Church. We are renting the building," May said. "They have even ordered new desks for us. It will be humble, but at least we will all be together again." She added that the school board was worried that the number of girls returning would be low, as some are being sent away to boarding schools.

I had to ask who, though the very idea filled me with dread. She said the Seawards had been to visit Ethel Pye and learned she is going to a school for young ladies in New Brunswick. Her father is a widower and he told them it will be a comfort to him to know she will have a solid roof over her head this winter, and easier for him to board as a bachelor. She's leaving soon.

Then May said, in a meaningful kind of way, "I'm afraid she may not be the only one. You *will* join us, Triffie, won't you?"

I told May how Papa feels about settling into our new neighbourhood. I didn't have to remind her of the parish school just by the Long Bridge. The truth is, I'm not sure where I'll be going to school in September, and that was all I could say.

May did not look happy, but she's the kind of girl who doesn't fuss. I used to be the kind who did, but I seem to be changing. When I look back now to the day when Alfie left, I can hardly believe the way I behaved.

But I didn't like to see May sad. I wasn't very happy myself, so I changed the subject, asking what she supposed would be in those boxes from London.

May told me she hoped there might be an every-day dress for her and I replied that this was exactly what I longed for as well, so I would not have to sit quietly in my rose satin every week while Nettie did the laundry.

"I'll wear it to the Regatta next week," I said, "but otherwise it's quite useless outside of Sundays."

"But, Triffie, there is no Regatta this year," May replied.

No Regatta! I couldn't believe it. They might as well cancel Christmas. "How can they take away the Regatta?" I thought of all the things we would miss. The boat races, the swings and tea tents. "Remember last year when Mr. Sainthill insisted he would walk the greasy pole out over the water, even though he was wearing a good suit?" We giggled as we pictured him sitting there soaking wet.

May told me Mr. Sainthill had lived at Avalon Cottage with them for a few weeks after the Clergy House burnt down, and he had been sent to Bonavista for the summer. We talked about him for a while, how funny he was with his proper English ways, but I couldn't stop thinking about the Regatta, and I had to ask May why it had been cancelled.

She reminded me of the people who are still living in tents on the field by the pond, then she put her hand on my arm. "Don't be sad, Triffie. I'm sure it will be back again next year."

By the time May left, I felt quite downcast. But I am determined now to make less trouble for everyone. When school starts back again, I'll do whatever Mama and Papa think best. The Regatta will be back next year and it wouldn't have been fun without Alfie anyway.

Wednesday, August 3rd, South Side Warehouse

I found a boy under the wharf! Sarah said it's just like finding a troll under a bridge, but Ned is nothing like a troll. I will tell the story properly.

I woke up early this morning, knowing there was a reason why, but I could not find it. Suddenly, I remembered — today should have been Regatta Day. I knew that if I stayed in bed I would just think on past Regatta Days until I'd made myself right glum, so I thought I might creep out and draw some water from the Critches' well — to make myself useful, as Nettie would say. I was rather proud to have such a practical thought, and even more pleased when I managed to dress, find the empty pail and get outside without disturbing anyone. I hoped to hear some praise at breakfast that might lift my spirits.

The night before, Papa had told us about the trouble over sheds that people are building at the public coves. Municipal Council approves, but the Premier said they are a disgrace and must be torn down at once. Now everyone is fighting about it. Papa says that people only want to live close to where they are working. He is also worried because more merchants are opening shops in sheds on Water Street. "Why would anyone pay for a cab to come over here when they can shop on Water Street?" he asked Mama. She wondered if Papa could make some kind of arrangement with Mr. Morrissey, but he said that would be too expensive to be practical.

Remembering all this, I took my pail to the wharf to see those new sheds across the water before I went to the well. It was windy enough that Regatta Day might have been postponed, and the harbour had a bit of a swell. As I stood there, I heard a knocking noise, as if something large was hitting the wooden pilings under me. Looking down at moving water makes me dizzy, so I lay flat on my tummy. Imagine my surprise when I saw a boy in a boat! It was a neat little boat, the kind we call a rodney. The boy was asleep, or so I thought, but when I looked at him, he opened his eyes. It was funny to watch his face go from calm and sleepy to terrified in just a few seconds. I don't believe I've ever frightened anyone in my life and

I wanted to tell him not to worry, but he spoke before I could.

"I'll be out of here the once, my maid," he said. "I never meant to trespass. I just needed a place to tie up for the night is all."

He spoke so nicely, I was sorry I'd frightened him. "Stay here as long as you please. I'm sure no one will mind." Then I wondered how anyone could live in a rowboat. "Are you hungry?" I asked.

He pointed to a little boarded-up compartment in the middle of his boat and I could hear the pride in his voice as he told me he'd stowed some bread from last night's supper midship to see him through the day. Then he noticed the pail and added, "I allow I could use a drink of water."

When he climbed up a little ladder at the side of the wharf, I found he stood head and shoulders above me. I guessed he was a little older than Sarah, about sixteen (which proved to be true). He wore a cloth cap with a peak. His arms and legs had grown a good few inches past the cuffs of his pants and jacket, which were frayed, but the way he took the pail for me made me think his manners better than many's a boy dressed in fine clothes.

I took him across the road to the Critches' garden, but he would not pass through the gate. "We'll be in for trouble if we trespasses," he said.

Sometimes in the street, I've passed a dog that has

a cruel master. You can tell these dogs by the mixture of fear and pleading in their eyes. I'm not especially fond of dogs, but that look tears at my heart. I saw that same look in this boy's eyes. I suddenly felt angry at whoever had put that whipped-dog look on his face, and my anger made me bold.

"We will not! Follow me." But he wouldn't. Luckily, Mr. Critch was enjoying his pipe in the garden. "Good morning, Mr. Critch," I called. "May we use your well?"

He laughed. "Triffie, maid, what are you on about? You knows you're welcome to our well."

When the boy heard this, he finally followed me. He drew the pail of water and drank by dipping his hand in, over and over again. Then he splashed it over his hair and face. I'd never seen anyone enjoy water so much. When he finished, he watered the Sweet William and Dame's Rocket growing near the well and drew a fresh pail for me. He looked ready to leave, but I was too curious to let him. I suggested we sit on the bench while he dried off. Then I introduced myself and asked him who he was.

"I'm Ned Shamler, Miss," he said, doffing his cap.

I asked him why he was sleeping in a rodney.

"That," he replied, "is a long story."

The sun had not yet crested the South Side hills behind us, and I knew it was still early. "No one needs this water yet," I told him. "I have time to listen."

I wasn't expecting a happy story, and it was not. Ned's parents both died of diphtheria when he was ten. His father had been a carpenter, but he'd broken his arm and it wasn't set properly, so after that, he could never work much. When his parents died, Ned was only able to keep out of the orphanage by begging his grandfather to take him in. "Grandfather took pity on me," he said. "But that was the first and only time." Ned had been going to the Springdale Street Mission School, which is free. He'd liked school, he told me, but that was the end of schooling for him. "Grandfather said it was time to make a man of me, and he had no objection to the money I earned him neither."

Ned went to work in the sail loft at the corner of Prescott and Duckworth Streets. Two years later, when his grandfather died, the owner let Ned sleep in the sail loft, but he docked a shilling off Ned's pay each week for that, though Ned couldn't say why. "The sails were there to sleep on and he never heated the place." Ned sighed. "The sail loft's gone now, though. Up in smoke, like the rest of the city." He told me that the rodney was the only thing he owned. His father had made it and Ned said he always managed to keep her on the water and get someone to help haul her out for the winter (calling the boat "her" as if it were his dearest friend). But then he stood up. "Your crowd will be after waking up about now. I'd best be on my way."

When I asked where he would go, he only shrugged.

Just then Mrs. Critch came out to draw some water. "Triffie, my darling, my hens has been laying their insides out. The eggs won't keep in this heat, and Nettie told me yesterday evening your stove's all set to go at last. Let me give you half a dozen so she can make a proper breakfast." Next thing I knew, she handed me a neat little basket.

I told Ned the eggs would never have come to us if I hadn't sat to listen to his story, and asked him to share our breakfast, but it was a job of work to make him agree. I finally had to tell him I couldn't carry the water and the eggs upstairs without his help.

By now everyone was up and dressed. I was wearing my everyday dress, with my pinafore over it, of course. It was one of my better everyday dresses, a pretty dark-blue cotton calico, but it's very plain and a pinny is a pinny. When Ned saw Mama and Papa in their fine clothes, he almost bolted, but I was behind and propelled him forward with only the tiniest shove as I presented the basket of eggs. Mrs. Critch's gift caused such celebration that Ned's presence was forgotten until, finally, Mama raised an eyebrow at me. I introduced Ned, stressing that we would not have gotten the eggs if not for him.

Nettie told us Mrs. Critch would know how to pickle eggs just as well as any woman, and these were given to us out of pure kindness. Then she whisked away to make us breakfast and Sarah followed, saying she would bring tea as soon as the kettle boiled. (The stove had finally been installed on the second floor yesterday evening after much grunting and hauling on ropes. Mr. Matt joked that they almost stove in the wall with the stove.)

I held my breath to see what would happen next. Before the fire, I knew, Mama would have given Ned a penny and dismissed him with a smile. But the fire had changed even Mama.

She told Ned that Nettie would not rest last night until she'd baked some bread, adding, "You helped Triffie find us a breakfast fit for kings. Stay and share our meal." But Mama was not entirely changed, because this was more of a command than an invitation, and Ned could not refuse, politely or otherwise. Some of us sat on our beds, some in barrel chairs. Mr. Matt joined us before the food appeared and quickly got Ned to talk about himself. Mama was shocked when Ned told them he'd been sleeping in his boat, but Papa was intrigued and he asked to see the boat after we'd finished breakfast. I could tell that Papa had a reason, but I had no clue what he was at.

The scrambled eggs were heavenly with fresh bread and butter. I never imagined food could taste so good. I could see Ned was puzzled by our fine china, so I leaned over and whispered, "These are our only dishes now. Mama saved them from the fire. The silver too."

As we ate, Papa raised his tea cup. "I propose a toast. To the stove, which rose like a phoenix from the ashes. Now that Nettie can cook again, our warehouse is truly a home."

"To the stove!" we cried, clinking our tea cups very, very carefully.

Ned stared as if we came from some strange country he could never have imagined, but he was smiling too.

Thursday, August 4th, South Side Warehouse

We are going to keep Ned! Papa looked at the boat and found it was sound. At once, he offered Ned a job with room and board. Sarah and I have been busy ever since, trying to make things comfortable for him at Mr. Matt's end of the floor. When we open our store, Ned's boat will ferry people across the harbour from the public cove at the bottom of Princes Street. Papa hopes customers will see a free boat ride as a treat. Some of Papa's other men will share the task of rowing so Ned doesn't wear himself out. There's room for two at the oars.

Ned still has the dazed look of someone who awoke to discover his life was only a bad dream. Tomorrow he'll row us across the harbour so we can visit Bannerman Park to see if we can find Miss Rosy and the others.

Friday, August 5th, South Side Warehouse

Today Mama is a heroine of the highest order. I think she even astonished herself. Soon I will tell the whole story, but for now I am writing quickly because Sarah and I must help Ned arrange a new bedroom with the crates he brought up through the receiving doors with the ropes and pulleys. Ned calls the doors "loopholes," and they are carefully barred with stout wooden boards when not in use, as they open onto thin air and it would be easy to fall from one. Papa and Mr. Matt made a bad job of it when they hoisted the stove to the second floor, but Ned learned to use the ropes and pulleys when he worked at the sail loft, and he's so clever, he can work all by himself.

After we arrange the room, Sarah and I are going outside to wait for Mr. Morrissey's cab to bring our dear shopgirls to us! We're so thrilled!

Details tomorrow, I promise!

Saturday, August 6th, South Side Warehouse

Finally we got a letter from Alfie yesterday, but it was as short as a telegram! *Everything nice here. Having fun. Your loving son, Alfred Winsor.*

Mrs. Parrott added a note to say that Alfie is a dear boy, that he fits right in and they have been taking good care of him. It was most unsatisfactory, and it made me miss Alfie all the more. Sarah and I will hardly know where to start when we write our next letter. So much has happened since Ned arrived! But I want to tell the story properly here and I began in the middle yesterday, so I'll go back now.

Yesterday afternoon Ned rowed us across the harbour so we could finally visit Bannerman Park. I mostly avoid looking at the north side now, but it loomed large in the boat. The fire stopped at the Bowring Brothers premises, which was partly burnt. I could see the scorch marks above one window on the eastern side, but from there west, the wharves and buildings along the waterfront are unchanged, even in places where the buildings behind, on Duckworth Street and the higher levels, were burnt to the ground. If I closed my left eye and looked to the right, the eastern side of the waterfront was all destruction. But, if I closed my right eye and looked left, the harbour looked as it always had.

At the public coves, men were busy building the very sheds the Government wants to tear down. We landed at the Fish Market at Clift's Cove, a wharf that wasn't as badly damaged as many. From there we walked through the heart of the destruction, confronting it at close hand for the first time.

The short street that leads from Clift's Cove to Water Street used to face the Market House, where we found men preparing to pull down remaining walls with ropes. Papa says, if the ropes are long enough to keep the men clear of the falling brick, this is not as dangerous as blasting powder. Soon after the fire, when the crew of the *Emerald* were blasting down the walls of the Athenaeum, some bricks flew through a window of the Union Bank next door and broken glass cut the manager where he sat in his parlour above the bank. It was one of the few buildings to survive the fire and it must have been a great shock for Mr. Goldie to be cut by flying glass in his own home.

As we walked through the ruined city, walls of empty shells rose around us like ghosts of the buildings they once were. "Imagine these streets at night with no street lamps," Sarah said with a shudder.

Mama led us straight up Cathedral Street. It was the most direct route out of the destruction, but it took us right past buildings that had been most dear to us.

The Cathedral stands roofless now and open to the sky, across from the remains of the well-built houses of Scotland Row. Only the stone wall and flagpole remain to show where Ashton Cottage stood on the other side of the street. Then we passed the site of our poor school, now just a few chimney towers, and climbed Garrison Hill, past pretty St. Patrick's Hall, which is also gutted. At Military Road the Roman Catholic Cathedral stood untouched and, for the first time, we saw green, living trees!

We all breathed easier with those charred ruins

behind us. Just before the park, we came to Rawlins Cross, where Mr. Rawlins' Grocery Store stood unchanged. On a whim, Mama took us in. "What do you suppose we might take to the park as a treat for the shopgirls we find there?" she asked, and we settled on some bottled lemonade which was chilling in a tub of ice water. As we left, Mr. Rawlins expressed his condolences for our losses.

Bannerman Park was transformed beyond recognition. The grass has been trampled away, leaving a field of beaten earth. Low, mean-looking sheds have sprung up in rows that face one another, with posts and a clothesline running between. In the distance, we saw larger makeshift buildings that must be the kitchens and hospital. Here, as everywhere else in the city, hammers pounded constantly in the background. It was like entering another world.

Mama has managed to dress much as she did before the fire, and Sarah and I wore everyday dresses without pinafores. Nettie keeps our clothing laundered and respectable, so no one seeing us for the first time would suspect our losses. A few women were standing in their doorways. Then I saw Susie's mother, Mrs. Verge, but she was busy with her children and didn't see me. I realized the Verges must have been here since the night of the fire. I tried to imagine such a large family living in one of these small sheds.

Next we passed a group of men who regarded us with open resentment as they puffed on their pipes. "They think we have come to gawk at their misfortune," Sarah whispered as we passed from one line of sheds to the next. Suddenly we found ourselves in the place the children had claimed for their playground. Some little girls were playing copyhouses with pieces of broken crockery and a doll that one of them must have kept with her the night of the fire. Others were skipping rope, and a group had formed a circle to play "Little Sally Saucer." It was just as bare and dusty here as everywhere else, but more cheerful.

As we passed some boys playing leapfrog, I recognized a little one who stood watching. "Look, Mama," I cried, "there's Georgie Ledwell!"

Georgie took us to his mother, who was sitting on a chair in the shade cast by her shed, hemming a blanket. She was cheerful about her family's prospects, telling us that Mr. Ledwell was already on the go at Courting Lane, working with a group of neighbourhood men who were helping one another rebuild in turn. "We hope to get clear of this place before the snow flies," she said. "These tilts got no floors in them, they was put up in such haste."

Now Sarah is calling me to come for a walk so we can show our dear shopgirls around the neighbourhood.

I will take up the story when we return.

Monday, August 8th
South Side Warehouse, just before dinner

Life is so lively here now, I find it hard to settle down and write! But I am determined to finish this story.

After we'd chatted with Mrs. Ledwell, she directed us to a small ring of tents near Rennie's Mill Road, "where they got the single ladies."

As we approached, someone called, "Oh, Mrs. Winsor!" and a young woman rushed from one of the tents to grasp Mama's hand. "Phoebe Dewling, Gloves," she said, to save Mama the embarrassment of not knowing her name, and I remembered how Phoebe had helped me pick my new summer gloves, back when such things still mattered. She even dropped a little curtsey. I hoped no one saw this. Mama is not the queen, after all.

Phoebe is a tall, thin girl with curly orange-coloured hair and a sprinkling of freckles across her long, narrow nose. She was kindly and high spirited in those golden days before the fire. But now, in spite of her nice manners, she was no longer one of Papa's smart shopgirls. The print blouse she wore was so large the sleeves began below her shoulders, and the hem of her skirt was edged with dust. Her head and hands were bare and there were dark circles under her eyes. Phoebe took us to a blanket beside the tent. The lemonade delighted her, but when we declined to share some, she put it away for later.

"I'm so glad we found you, Phoebe," Mama said. "Are others here as well?"

Phoebe knew Mama was asking about Papa's crowd. "Three of us lives here, Mrs. Winsor, ma'am. Liza Tizzard and myself are both from Greenspond, but they had the diphtheria some bad there in the spring, so we'd rather take our chances here." She went on to tell us that Liza was one of Mrs. Steele's tailoresses. "God love Mrs. Steele," she added. "Her little house over on Maxse Street is full to the brim with her girls. She offered to squeeze Liza in somehow, but Liza and myself has always been fast friends and she couldn't bear leave me here."

Mama patted her hand and told her Liza sounded like a faithful companion.

Phoebe nodded. "She is, Mrs. Winsor. She and Miss Rosy are over to the Relief Stores at the Parade Street Rink now. We hear they got some mattresses and we're tired of sleeping on the ground." Then she began to explain how difficult the relief system was, how beset with paperwork and waiting, both here at the Colonial Building at the edge of the park where the relief orders are handed out, then at the Parade Rink, where the relief is stored and distributed.

As she explained, she grew more agitated. "It's not a long walk from here to Fort Townsend, but they keeps you outside in all weather. Outside! No one can say why — there's plenty of room in the curling rink. We take turns, lining up for hours and hours over there, but one of us always stays here to stand guard." She lowered her voice. "You can't blink in this place, Mrs. Winsor. Miss Rosy washed her one good blouse when they put up the first clothesline and it was gone five minutes later."

Mama asked Phoebe if they'd been sleeping here since the fire. She may have been trying to calm her by changing the subject, but the misery of living in the park was exposed at every turn. Phoebe told us they'd slept out under the open sky for the first few nights, until the tents had arrived. She wrung her hands and explained that families were given tilts first, so single girls might have to wait weeks for one.

"People say, why don't you ship out to Canada or Boston? We could get free passage, but none of us can bear the thought of leaving." Phoebe's sharp chin went up as she told us there was no respect for single, working women in the park, adding, "I can't count the times we've been told we should find ourselves husbands." When Miss Rosy complained to a Constabulary officer after her blouse disappeared, he'd said it would never have happened if she had a husband to protect her. "'Plenty of able-bodied bachelors living in the park,' he'd told her. 'Take your pick.'" And everyone who'd gathered to listen just laughed.

I could hardly believe my ears.

"Could you imagine anyone talking like that to Miss Rosy before the fire?" Phoebe asked.

She lowered her voice, although there was no one near, and told us Miss Rosy could have gone to live with people on her staff. "I think she stayed because she was sure young Mr. Waldegrave would come to her rescue," she continued. "His people got a big, fine house just over on Monkstown Road. But next we heard, he's off to Boston without so much as goodbye. Miss Rosy's trying to keep her spirits up, same as Liza and me, but that laid her low, it truly did."

The indignities they'd had to bear seemed endless, Phoebe told us. One of the worst happened the week before, when *The Morning Despatch* printed a story about a farmer in Maine who'd written to the Mayor, saying he'd be happy to take in a young woman as a domestic, and if they got along, he'd marry her. He'd meant it as a way of providing relief, Phoebe said, but it got written up in *The Despatch* as a kind of joke. Unfortunately, her friend Liza Tizzard happened to match the man's description of his ideal woman — "Plump and light-complected." Now, whenever she walks in the park, someone will yell, "There goes a plump and light-complected woman. Get her on the first boat out to Maine." She shook her head as she told us. "Liza can take a joke as well as anyone, but all this misfortune got us worn down and it brings her close to tears, it really do."

As Mama listened, she seemed to grow, as if she were actually filling with indignation. "We cannot have this!" she said when Phoebe finished, and she announced that the three of them must pack up their things so we could put a roof over their heads "this very night." I'd never imagined she'd do anything so magnificent!

Phoebe's mouth fell open for a long moment, then she threw herself into Mama's arms and began to sob. If Mama had told her she was condemned to hang by the neck until dead, she could not have cried harder. People passing by cast looks of sympathy our way, imagining Phoebe had just received some tragic news. When she finally composed herself, she apologized, begging us to stay and tell Liza and Miss Rosy the good news.

But Mama had other plans. She stood, telling Phoebe we needed to go tell Papa so he could arrange for a cab to collect them. She tried to warn her that our warehouse is very humble, but Phoebe rose as well, grasping Mama's hand again. "Just to find ourselves in polite company again will make it a palace."

We took our leave, but every time I looked back, Phoebe was still watching and, each time, she waved again.

As we left the park, I had a thought. "Now that Mr. Waldegrave is gone, Miss Rosy and Mr. Matt can be sweethearts again."

Mama stopped walking. "Oh dear. I quite forgot about that. Poor Matthew."

"But, Mama, they cared about one another once, why can't Miss Rosy just unjilt him?" I asked.

Mama sighed and said a man was unlikely to forgive such a slight. She was sorry to be throwing them together like this, but the deed was done. Then she took each of us by the hand and asked us how we thought Papa was going to greet our news.

"He will be pleased, Mama," Sarah said. "You acted so nobly. How could we have left three of his crowd in such misery?"

Mama smiled and said she hoped Sarah was right.

And, of course, she was.

Thursday, August 11th, South Side Warehouse

Though it's mid-afternoon, I've had to pull a barrel chair over to the window to get enough light to write, it's that dark today. But we are in no way downcast by the weather, for it feels as if a small flock of good fairies has descended upon our home. Miss Rosy, Phoebe and Liza spend a good part of the day singing as they bustle around, transforming everything. Phoebe, who has little sisters at home in Greenspond, takes great delight in dressing my hair, and she's so clever that Nettie says I no longer look like a birch broom in the fits.

It was lucky we rescued them because it began to

pour yesterday, and the rain shows no sign of letting up. Their tent would have been miserable by now. They cannot stop exclaiming over their good fortune.

When we told Papa, he looked astonished for an instant, then began to plan with enthusiasm, saying they must have their own "room" made of old crates to give them privacy.

Papa has been buying bits of furniture from our neighbours on the South Side. Sarah and I now share a cast-iron bedstead with a proper mattress and we even have our own washstand. I told Papa that we had already decided we would give that washstand to the three young ladies.

He smiled and promised to make arrangements with Mr. Morrissey to transport them, adding, "The timing is excellent, because I have some good news." Then he told us a telegram had reached him this morning, and a cargo ship, the SS *Fez*, will arrive the week of the fifteenth with a shipment of goods for us. "So we can put those girls to work quite soon," he concluded. Since the store's records were lost in the fire, no one knows what's in the shipment, but as Papa said, anything will be welcome.

Sarah and I told Ned our exciting news as he rowed us across the harbour. When we reached the warehouse, Nettie had fresh raisin buns waiting. Of course, we had to tell the story all over again to her, so no one noticed that Ned had disappeared until we heard the ropes moving in their pulleys outside. While we were enjoying our raisin buns, he had taken old crates out by the wharf, dusted them off and prepared to haul them up to our attic. He cleverly packed smaller crates inside the largest ones and, in no time, we had enough crates to lay out a good-sized "room" for our dear shopgirls. (I know Miss Rosy is not a shopgirl, or Liza Tizzard for that matter, but I cannot write, "Papa's head milliner, tailoress and glove-counter girl" every time I refer to them.)

Sarah and I helped Ned to place the crates around a dormer window in the middle of the warehouse to give the "room" some light. He showed us how to stack smaller ones onto larger ones so there was no danger of the "walls" tipping. With our washstand inside and beds made from boards and straw pallets, it looked almost cozy. With Mama's permission, Ned nailed the edge of a thin blanket between two planks and we placed this over the entrance for privacy. Nettie had managed to get some salt beef and she said she would cook up a proper boiled dinner to celebrate.

Then Sarah and I went to sit by the Critches' to watch for the carriage, which finally crossed the Long Bridge, raising a cloud of dust as it came toward us. Papa sat in front with Mr. Morrissey. Miss Rosy jumped out almost before the carriage came to a proper stop and rushed over to hug us. Like Phoebe and Liza, she looked much reduced in ill-fitting hand-me-downs, but we all beamed as we led our dear shopgirls upstairs. They greeted the humble space we had prepared for them as if it were a suite in the finest hotel, and when we told them how hard Ned had worked to make it ready, they praised him until he grew quite red. Then they unpacked their few things and declared themselves to be in heaven.

Mr. Matt returns from work earlier now, as the need for new stovepipes is easing, and I noticed he was not nearly as pleased as everyone else to discover the new additions to our household. I wondered if sharing the same roof with Miss Rosy would make him sad, and it was hard not to stare at him. When our fine meal was finished, Mr. Matt immediately said he could use some fresh air and would Ned mind a row around the harbour? Ned did not mind. (He is very much in awe of Mr. Matt and seems astonished by his friendship.) So off they went.

Phoebe and Liza refused to let Nettie touch the dishes that night and in the days that have followed. Nettie grumbles that she will be out of a job if the cargo ship does not arrive soon, but I believe she is secretly pleased to be treated so well. Liza sews gentlemen's and boys' clothing. This is skilled work and she lamented the loss of her sewing machine while doing the dishes that first night, saying she could easily take Phoebe's blouse in if only she had a needle and some pins.

"I have my needle case," I told her, "but I've only got embroidery silks."

Sarah added that she had spools of thread, her needle case and her pincushion, "along with all my hat trimmings."

That delighted Miss Rosy, of course, who asked Papa what had become of the supplies she rescued the day of the fire. Papa told her that Mr. Morrissey had brought everything saved from the fire with him on the day we moved here and the boxes were stowed on the second floor. Miss Rosy instantly jumped up and took Sarah off with her to have a look.

Then Phoebe told Liza she'd finish the dishes so Liza could sew. "If you can make this blouse more becoming," she said, "I'll give you my first-born child."

Liza laughed. "I'll fix your blouse and welcome, but I'd just as soon pass on your first-born child."

After Liza had looked through our sewing supplies, Mama was forced to admit I wasn't quite as impractical as she had declared me to be that afternoon in Mrs. Sampson's garden. Phoebe changed into her one good blouse and soon Liza was busy attacking the oversized hand-me-down with needle and pins, and it looks much better now.

Friday, August 12th, South Side Warehouse

Our dear shopgirls brought a stack of the past few weeks' newspapers with them from the park, but we were too busy to look at them until today, when Miss Rosy, Phoebe and Liza disappeared for the day. They still have their relief orders for mattresses, and they are determined to replace the straw pallets if they can. Having slept on those pallets, no one can blame them. Standing in line outside the Parade Rink is so tedious that they decided they would all go. As they left, Phoebe said it was a joy to know their possessions would be safe while they were gone.

The rain has stopped, but it feels as if Miss Rosy, Phoebe and Liza took all our sunshine with them when they left today. I confess I had not fully understood how very much they have cheered us until they were gone. Sarah and I took to the newspapers to distract ourselves from the empty feeling that filled the warehouse, and soon Mama joined us.

Perhaps it's not strange to find we were all most interested in news of property stolen the night of the fire. Mama read that the police had made a raid on Quidi Vidi Village, recovering a large quantity of stolen goods soon after the fire. "That must ease Mr. Morrissey's mind considerably," she said.

I noticed an item about men who had been convicted for stealing carpets and tea chests, then Sarah began to read a story from *The Despatch* about a man who had been sentenced to six months for stealing a piano out of a house on Carter's Hill the night of the fire.

"A piano!" Mama exclaimed. "Just imagine the effort it would take to steal a piano."

I said nothing, but my heart leapt up. If a piano was snatched from the fire, anything might have been saved, no matter how big.

Sarah read on and it was an interesting story. The piano was recovered because of a plainclothes policeman who had been at work in town even before the fire happened. "Due to the efforts of this constable, a great quantity of valuable property has been recovered and now lies in Fort Townsend, awaiting owners," Sarah read. I could tell from her face that her thoughts were the same as mine.

Mama wondered how a policeman could manage to work in plain clothes without detection in St. John's. She concluded that perhaps they had brought the constable in especially, as most Constabulary officers are known by name in this city. It seemed to me she could have shown more interest in the furniture.

Then I found a notice in *The Despatch* which I read aloud. It was of such interest to us all, I'm going to copy it out. It reads as follows:

> DELIVER! All persons who have saved property from the late fire in Saint John's, and now have such property in their possession without authority, are required

immediately to deliver such property to the Police Barracks, Fort Townsend, and to give all necessary information concerning the same.

All persons found hereafter in possession of such property, or who do not immediately obey this order, will be prosecuted with the utmost rigor of the law.

All questions of bona fide salvage claims in respect to such property will be investigated by the undersigned Magistrates and promptly disposed of.

D.W. Prowse and J.G. Conroy,
Stipendiary Magistrates for
Newfoundland, Fishermen's and
Seamen's Home, July 21, '92

After I read this out, Sarah asked Mama, was there any chance of us recovering some of our furniture? But Mama said we should not pin our hopes on such an unlikely event. "Those things are gone," she added. "We survived without injury, and one day soon we will all be together again. That should be enough for us."

But I cannot help wondering if our fine furniture is somewhere in this city, sitting in a stranger's house.

Sunday, August 14th, South Side Warehouse

Today being Sunday, we ran out of ways to amuse ourselves and talk turned to the day of the fire. It seems enough time has passed that we can speak freely of it now without renewing the fear and horror of the day. Phoebe and Liza told us how bold Miss Rosy was when she defended Mr. Morrissey's cab against the looters, and it was clear that Miss Rosy liked to hear the story again. Her cheeks took on fresh colour and I could well imagine how fearsome she must have seemed. Next, Mr. Matt told us how Papa's crowd organized themselves into a fire brigade, all hands standing ready with buckets full of water while the fire advanced upon the harbour. The flankers that first landed on the wooden windowsills were easily extinguished, but when the tar on the roof caught fire — not once but often — he said, "We knew we were sunk."

Then Ned began his tale. When the City Hall Skating Rink was set alight by flaming debris, he knew the sail works was bound to follow, for it was downwind and just across Prescott Street. "Most of the houses uphill was all aflame," he told us, "and I thought of my rodney." So off he went to the public cove where he kept his prize possession. He rowed it across the harbour and moored on the South Side. At first, he was terrified he'd see people burning to death, but when this didn't happen he began to realize that they were keeping out of the fire's path, so it wasn't as terrible as he'd expected. He stayed there all night, watching. "I still sees it when I close my eyes before sleep," he said. "Showers of flankers lashing across the harbour like a curtain of glowing, orange snow."

As he watched, building after building caught fire, burned and collapsed onto itself and the east side of the city was reduced to smoldering ashes. "By the time the sun came up," he said, "I thought my life would never be the same." But then he smiled. I think he smiled because he was right, but in a happy way. Without the fire, we'd never have met Ned.

I'm glad he's come to live with us now, and I believe he feels the same way about us.

So many tales of bravery and daring were told this afternoon, I only wish Alfie had been at my side to hear them.

Monday, August 15th, South Side Warehouse

I am so very worried, I must record my fears here to quiet them. This is an unsettled time for everyone. Miss Rosy and Sarah are the only lucky ones. They have set up a millinery workshop for themselves and they spend their time working on "the fall line of hats," but the rest of us can only wait for the SS *Fez* to arrive with new stock so we can open our shop.

Today I found myself alone with nothing to do.

Ned had taken Liza and Phoebe across the harbour so they could visit Liza's friends at Mrs. Steele's house in Georgestown. After they left, I could not sit still to watch the hat making. Nettie was busy kneading bread, and soon tired of watching me prowl around looking for something to do. "You're all at sixes and sevens today," she said, and told me I'd better get myself outside. I didn't even wonder where Mama and Papa had gone.

There's a small patch of bare land beside the warehouse near the wharf. I was looking for a stone there, so I could draw some hopscotch squares, when I heard voices and realized that Mama and Papa were close by, sitting on a bench facing the water just around the corner. I didn't mean to eavesdrop, but I stood there frozen, listening to them.

Papa said the new street lines for Water and Duckworth Streets are to be published any day now and there will soon be auctions of new bricks, but how, he asked, can bricks be laid in freezing weather. He grew more and more agitated as he went on to say that the Royal Engineers are waiting in Halifax to come and help lay out the streets, but they cannot because new barracks must be built for them at Fort Townsend, and that's taking longer than expected. At this rate, no start will be made on our new store until next spring. Then he wondered how "the girls" will accept the plan that he proposes. Mama replied that we'd been brave since the fire, and she was sure we'd continue to be, no matter what.

At that, I turned and fled, and nothing Nettie said could make me go outside again. I finally had to take up Sarah's copy of that wretched *Wuthering Heights,* which I'd abandoned weeks before, so I could brood in peace.

What did Papa mean? I thought back to the conversation May and I had, just before I found Ned, and my heart froze. Papa couldn't possibly mean to send us away to school, could he?

Tuesday, August 16th, South Side Warehouse

I stayed very close to Sarah today. A sleepless night knocked all the restlessness out of my limbs, and I feel better when she is near, so I took my Fancy Needlework down to the millinery workshop, although I did very little sewing. Miss Rosy soon remarked that I was yawning to split my face, but Sarah chatted away while they worked, without a care in the world.

Papa came by at one point and paused to watch us sewing together with such a tender look, almost as if he were trying to fix us in his memory. When he was gone, I moved so close to Sarah that she had to ask me to give her a little elbow room, please, so I put my sewing away and brought my writing desk down here.

I am certain now that he and Mama have decided to send us away to a boarding school.

Oh, Papa is calling us now. How can I bear this?

Later in the evening

I am so very happy! Everything is fine, although I wouldn't have guessed it when Papa asked Sarah and me to come outside with him and Mama so we could have a private conversation. I feared the worst as they led us to the same bench where I had overheard them talking yesterday, and Papa's grim frown did nothing to reassure me.

He said it was time to talk about the future, and we were faced with some serious decisions. He wanted Sarah and me to understand why he and Mama have chosen to do things as they are to be done. I *knew* they had decided to send Sarah and Alfie and me away to boarding school just like Ethel Pye. I had to will myself not to burst into tears.

Then Papa said, "We have decided a new store must be our first priority. Once other shops are properly restored on Water Street, our trade here is bound to suffer. So we will put off building a new house until our shop reopens at the old premises. It may take more than a year, or even two, before we have a house again. I know this must be a terrible disappointment," he continued, but I could not hold my tongue another second.

"But we will remain together?" I asked.

"Together?" Mama said. "Why Triffie, of course."

I threw myself into Mama's arms and the tears I had been trying to hold back burst from me in a torrent. It was some time before I could explain myself.

I was not scolded for eavesdropping. (It was, after all, an accident.)

"My goodness, Triffie," Mama said, "Mr. Pye's situation is quite different, being a widower without property."

"But many good families do send their children away for school," Sarah said, and she confessed that the thought had crossed her mind as well. (If only I'd known, I could have shared my worries.)

"My dear girls!" Papa cried. "Never! Without you, our hearts would be quite broken. It's been hard enough to do without Alfie for so long."

Mama added it was time for Alfie to come home and she was composing a wire that will go the clergyman in Scilly Cove this coming week, asking him to arrange a passage for Alfie and Ruby. "Alfie must be here before school starts in September," she concluded.

I was so happy and relieved and thought it just as well to get my worries all clewed up at the same time. "And will we go to St. Mary's School?" I asked.

Mama said, "Of course not, Triffie. You and Sarah will return to the Church of England Girls'

School," and she told us Alfie will begin his studies at the Church of England Academy — which, by luck, is just a short distance from St. Thomas, where our school is to be. So everything works out just as I wished! We talked quite happily about our future. Papa said he felt a great weight had been removed from his shoulders to know that Sarah and I are content to remain here, however long it may take to build a new house.

I am quite content to stay here. In fact, I would miss Ned and Phoebe and Liza and Miss Rosy and Mr. Matt very much. I can't wait to tell May we'll be back together in the fall. Perhaps I will write her a postcard!

Thursday, August 18th, South Side Warehouse

We have been so busy this week, it's hardly the same place. Papa's first shipment of goods arrived on Tuesday morning. The SS *Fez* is a big iron steamship and it loomed large as it docked at our wharf. We watched, safe and dry inside, as the men unloaded our goods in the pouring rain. Papa's order was just a small part of the cargo, so it did not take long for the crates and one large barrel to be landed on the wharf. Then the ship sailed along the South Side to the Job Brothers' warehouse.

The rain had kept Papa home and it was funny to watch him take orders from Ned, but he's the only one here who knows how to handle cargo. Afterwards Papa said we are lucky to have him. I'm sure Alfie would have enjoyed learning to use the ropes and pulleys. I can't wait for him to be with us again.

When everything was safely stowed on the second floor, Papa insisted we eat dinner before opening the crates. It was noon and Nettie had a nice pea soup with dumplings ready, and, as Papa said, he and Ned needed to dry out as much as the cargo did.

We could barely contain ourselves while we ate. It felt like Christmas morning and our dear shopgirls were just as eager as Sarah and I. We spent the whole meal talking about what we most wanted to find in the crates. Miss Rosy wanted more millinery supplies, of course, and Liza still longs for a sewing machine. Papa told her, if he had only known he was about to lose them all, he would certainly have ordered one last May when this order was placed. Phoebe said she'd be pleased to sell anything. "I still dream that I'm standing behind my counter, in a crisp white blouse and neat serge skirt with rows and rows of lovely gloves under the glass in front of me."

Liza said, "Well girl, we'll be on the go again just as soon as we gets everything arranged. You'll have to teach me how to manage like a shopgirl."

Papa said he hoped it would stop raining. As soon as he had a list of the goods we have to sell, he planned to go over to Monroe's wharf where *The*

Morning Despatch is printed to submit a shop opening announcement to that paper. "And that should get us started."

I asked if he would tell people that Ned will row them across to us, and he laughed and said he wouldn't be putting it quite that way. Then he asked for our opinion of the wording. "How's this? 'Water cab service across the harbour offered to all customers, free of charge'?"

Sarah said it sounded as if Papa had hired a Victoria cab to float across the harbour. Ned wondered if people would be disappointed "when they sees my old rodney."

Mama told him that it was part of our trade to make people believe something they might take for granted is actually quite wonderful. "I'm sure your neat little rodney will delight everyone," she added.

By then our bowls were empty and I could wait no longer. "Papa," I said, "we have been very patient and you look quite dry — "

I got no farther because everyone burst out laughing.

"You *have* been patient," Papa said, throwing down his napkin.

As we rose from the table, Phoebe began to gather the plates. Nettie insists on eating after us now, as she did before the fire. She was sitting by the window, waiting for us to finish, and she spied Phoebe right away. "What do you think you're at, Miss?"

Phoebe replied that dinner had been so fine, she felt she should help with the dishes. Anyone could see what a sacrifice this was for her. Luckily, Nettie wouldn't hear of it.

"Go on with your foolishness. Time for you to get back to your proper work, and me to mine." And Nettie shooed us toward the stairs. Even Mama came down to help.

The second floor is cozy. The stove keeps the damp off, and we've swept it clean. Phoebe and Liza even washed all the little windows with vinegar and newspaper soon after they arrived, so it's almost bright. Ned began to open the crates with an old pry bar that Papa had discovered on the first floor. When he was done, he went down to the ground floor to find more empty crates that might serve as shop counters.

We fell upon the contents of the first crates with cries of delight. Inside we found ready-made winter fashions for ladies: coats and dresses, skirts and blouses. Mama said that she thought we could spare a good set of clothes for Liza, Phoebe and Rose, adding, "After all, our shop must look smart."

"Oh, thank you, Mrs. Winsor," Phoebe cried, running her hand over a neat dress of navy crepe. Her eyes shone. Miss Rosy thanked Mama too, but she wasn't about to let anything slow us down, saying they'd see about that after we finished working. There were crates of yard goods and even some gloves to make Phoebe happy, but no clothes for girls. I tried to hide my disappointment. I would like to have a new dress too. Then we opened a small crate filled with bars of Castile soap and *eau de cologne.*

"Now *this* is bound to be popular," Miss Rosy said, "with everyone needing a bath."

Mama agreed, but added that we'll be needing a sign that reads *At Greatly Reduced Price*s as fancy soaps and scent will not be at the top of shopping lists now. This caused Papa to remark that Mama is "every inch the businesswoman," and she glowed to hear his praise.

Miss Rosy was transported by joy when we opened the next crate, as it was filled with millinery supplies. She ran her hands over the bolts of felt, the packets of feathers, velvet flowers and ribbons as if they were the riches of the earth, promising to make Liza into a milliner while she was waiting for a sewing machine.

The next crates were full of men's and boys' shoes. "So," Papa said, "we only have ladies' fashions and men's shoes." He hoped another shipment would arrive soon to fill the gaps in our stock.

Next we opened two smaller crates. One held watches and jewellery, and the other knives. Papa said the knives are probably more valuable than jewellery now.

When I asked if we'd be changing our prices to

reflect this, Papa was scandalized. "That, Triffie my love, is called profiteering," and he explained that merchants must never make profit out of misfortune caused by disaster or war, calling this "one of the graver sins of commerce." I was mortified to have made such a mistake, but he patted me on the head when he finished, to show my ignorance had not offended him (and now I know better). Papa went on to say, when the shop opening announcement is printed, it will state *All Goods Offered at Pre-Fire Prices*, so everyone will know we are honest traders.

The last crate was filled with package upon package of small paper bags. "Candy bags," Mama said. And we were all silent for a moment, remembering our fine candy kitchen.

As if he'd read everyone's mind, Papa said, "This place is not clean enough for a candy kitchen." Then he pointed to a barrel as tall as I am and sighed. "Only the hogshead left. I'm afraid I know what's inside." It was filled with sugar, the entire winter's supply for the confectionery.

"My goodness," Mama said. "That's a grand lot of sugar. How much, exactly?"

"One thousand, five hundred pounds," Papa replied. "It's cheaper to buy this way."

We stood in silent awe for a moment, then a giggle escaped Mama. Miss Rosy pressed her hand to her mouth, but she too succumbed to giggles. The silliness of all that sugar was too much for us. We laughed until our sides ached and tears ran down our cheeks.

"Oh dear," Mama said when she was finally able to catch her breath. "What will we do with it all?"

Papa replied that in time he would try to find a place to rent so we can get the candy kitchen on the go once more, but he was more interested in getting the shop opened just now. Then he and Mama went to compose the shop opening announcement, leaving us to lay out the shop. While we were busy with the new stock, Ned had carried up enough crates for us to make a start on our counters, and Miss Rosy was eager to take the space in hand. While Phoebe, Liza and Miss Rosy planned the layout of our shop, I went to the crate of soap and picked up a bar, so pretty in its fancy paper wrapping. I closed my eyes and breathed in the soapy scent. It smelled so clean, so unlike the stink of ashes and fish and rotting cod livers that clings to us now. It smelled of the life we've lost.

I try not to dwell upon the past, to be content with our new life, but just for a moment, I wished us back in Papa's store, with everything so clean and orderly, just as it had been before the fire snatched it all away. I wished so hard, my eyeballs hurt. When I opened my eyes, Sarah was watching me. She put her arm around me and gave me a little squeeze. "Come now, Triff. Just think how happy Alfie will be when he gets home and finds we are open for business again."

That cheered me. The makeshift counters are laid out in a large U now, with plenty of space to store stock behind. The shop is neat and ready for customers. By Monday, we'll be open.

Saturday, August 20th, South Side Warehouse

Mama and Papa spent all of yesterday in our new shop, entering the stock into an inventory book, which must be done before goods can be sold. Mr. McAllister generally keeps track of inventory for Papa, but he is still on holiday in Scotland. While they worked, Mama's thoughts strayed again and again to the sugar and what a waste it seemed to have so much when others had none at all. The only other useless items were the candy bags.

Then, in what Papa calls a flash of genius, Mama realized we could put the two together. So when the shop opening announcement ran today, it not only said, *Water cab service across the harbour offered to all customers, free of charge from the public cove, foot of Princes Street,* and *All goods offered at pre-fire prices,* it also read, *A packet of sugar with all purchases, gratis.*

Sarah and I spent a good part of today filling small candy bags with sugar, using a soup ladle that Nettie saved from the fire. I am too tired to write more.

Sunday, August 21st, South Side Warehouse

After working so hard yesterday, we were glad to take our day of rest and assembled for church in excellent cheer. Our dear shopgirls looked much improved, and only slightly overheated in their new winter outfits. Only one small thing marred an otherwise perfect day. Phoebe and Liza proposed to cross the Long Bridge on foot, as George Street Wesleyan Church lies just beyond. When they told us this, Mr. Matt said, "I hear the parson gives a right good sermon at that church. I believe I'll accompany you ladies, if you've no objection." Mr. Matt follows the Church of England. He was part of our congregation at the Cathedral until the fire.

Phoebe and Liza were delighted, of course. Miss Rosy said nothing, but I saw a look of utter dismay flash across her face. She is also Church of England (her Sunday bonnets caused such a sensation that Mama used to joke that ladies from other churches would attend our services just to see them). Miss Rosy quickly composed herself and no one else saw, but I do believe she is very sorry now that she threw Mr. Matt over and would willingly be his sweetheart again, if he would only give her the chance. But I don't think he will, because I've noticed that he never addresses Miss Rosy directly and he will look anywhere to avoid meeting her eyes.

We all set off together, Miss Rosy chatting to Sarah

with great animation about the hats they were making. I think she was trying to show that Mr. Matt's attentions mean nothing to her now, but I do not believe this. It's an unhappy situation.

After noontime dinner, we would willingly have gone downstairs to fuss over the store, but that, sadly, would count as work. Liza proposed a walk, but Miss Rosy said she had a headache and took to her bed. It must have been a terrible headache, for she looked miserable. Liza and Phoebe and Mr. Matt and Ned set off together and I sat down to make this quick entry in my diary. Now Sarah and I will settle down to write our last weekly letter to Alfie, though it may not reach him before he comes home! I wish he had written us once more. I allow it must be an effort for him to write anything, but I do hope he hasn't forgotten me.

Tuesday, August 23rd
Winsor & Son Mercantile Premises

The store opening was such a grand success, it left us quite exhausted. Luckily, today is a bank holiday, to make up for the holiday we missed on Regatta Day, so we can rest. Nettie is packing a picnic and we're all going to walk along South Side Road the whole way to Fort Amherst at the mouth of the Narrows, where the fresh salt air will revive us, no doubt. But before we go, I want to write about our opening day.

The boat ride proved to be a grand inducement, and Ned told us of customers lined up at the public cove, waiting their turns. Others came by carriage and a good many walked. The South Side has grown (as have all the neighbourhoods that survived the fire) so we have plenty of local customers. But the fire has changed the harbour too. There are so many ships now, delivering aid and mail from Canada, the United States and Britain, that it is almost dangerous to take a small boat like Ned's rodney across.

Ned said he would be fine, but Papa insisted that Mr. Stabb himself row as well, as he is the one with the most ship sense. I could tell Ned found Mr. Stabb a bit frightening, as Alfie and I always have, and he was quite dwarfed by our wharf master when they rowed side by side, but at the end of the day, Mr. Stabb said Ned was a dab hand with an oar, giving him a slap on the back that pretty nearly decked him. Ned seemed delighted, as he always is when anyone is kind to him. I'm pleased to note that the whipped-dog expression is fading from his eyes.

The sugar was another reason we attracted so many customers, just as Mama planned. Papa is sure we saw more trade because of it.

Now everyone is getting ready, and I must go find my hat.

Thursday, August 25th
Winsor & Son Mercantile Premises

The shop is so busy, I have little time to write. Today we finally had a second letter from Alfie, but it was just like the first. It's been very vexing to hear so little from him! But we also had a wire from Scilly Cove, telling us that Ruby and Alfie are to return a week this Saturday aboard a schooner with the unlikely name of *Prince Le Boo*. Everyone else will welcome Ruby, but I am still angry with her. Without her interference, Alfie would not have gone so far, or for such a long time. I have missed him fiercely. I would like to be able to forgive her, but I don't believe I am good enough to do so.

Friday, August 26th
Winsor & Son Mercantile Premises

We had scarcely finished breakfast this morning when a steamer called with a second shipment of stock. As we tried to unpack and mind the store at the same time, Papa said it was time to start hiring again, so he's going to put the word out among his crowd. These crates were mostly filled with kitchenware and crockery, which pleased Papa because these goods are in great demand as people restock their cupboards. He promptly made Mama the gift of a set of everyday dishes, so now we'll eat off ordinary Blue Willow plates again. It took us most of the day to unpack the crates between the jigs and the reels, because we had to keep stopping to help customers. Mama says she and Papa will burn the midnight oil tonight, doing the inventory so the new goods can go out tomorrow.

In the middle of everything, Miss Maude Seaward arrived with our poor box from London, giving Ned a penny when he carried it up for her. Mama offered her tea, but she could see how busy we were and she had other boxes to deliver, so she didn't stay. Afterwards, we were glad she wasn't there when we finally unpacked the poor box behind the counters among the new crates, because our anticipation soon turned to dismay. As Miss Rosy later said, poor was the best word for that box indeed. She and Phoebe and Liza did nothing but laugh at the clothes, but they may. August has turned wet and cool, so they are more comfortable in the warmer ladies' clothes that arrived in the first shipment. They look quite fashionable again, but it's another matter for me.

Mama unpacked one disappointment upon the next — threadbare skirts, yellowed blouses, frayed sweaters. The best thing for me was a faded gingham pinafore which I can at least use to protect my everyday dress. The white pinny I wore the day of the fire is quite worn out now from constant wear. The worst thing was a dress my size, dark mauve satin, all flounces and frills. It would have been hideous when new, but someone had spilled a cup of tea across the front, leaving a pattern of splashes, big and small. The thought of wearing it brought tears to my eyes.

"Oh dear," Mama said.

Liza picked it up, weighing the fabric with expert hands. "This would make lovely pincushions," she said, "if I cut around the marred parts and unpick the lace for trim."

Mama gave my shoulder a little pat. "Yes, Liza, please do. Not all charity is kind."

The next thing that came out of the box was wonderful, though not for me. It was a brown flannel suit, well cut, for a young man. We were astonished because Ned did not come to live with us until after May's family came to visit that Sunday. Nettie says it was providential. (If so, I must be out of favour with Providence these days.)

"Why, it's hardly been worn," Liza said when she saw the suit. "Ned! Where're you to? Get yourself over here."

The jacket sleeves and pant legs were a little long, but otherwise the suit fit Ned perfectly. "You looks every inch the gentleman in that outfit." Liza said. "Just let me pin the cuffs."

We flattered Ned that much, he turned quite pink. I'm sure he was glad when we finished, but his eyes shone when he looked at the suit on Liza's arm.

The box was nearly empty now, but we found a

woollen shawl that will suit Nettie, and some knitted scarves and stockings with hardly any holes. Finally, at the bottom of the box, there was a dress for Sarah that Mama pronounced "perfectly serviceable." It's grey linsey-woolsey, or "wincey" as Liza says, with handmade lace at the collar and cuffs, and only a few moth holes. Mama is darning them now.

"It is a bit old-fashioned," Miss Rosy said when Sarah modelled it for us. "All those flounces at the back might as well be a bustle, but never mind. A few rows of narrow black velvet ribbon just above the hem and cuffs would make it more fashionable." And Liza agreed.

With that, the box was empty and we were glad. Mama remarked that we'd now have excellent cleaning rags. Ned's suit was the only truly good thing in it. As Phoebe says, he will look "a right perfect gentleman" come Sunday morning.

So it was a day of surprises, and most of them unpleasant, but the nicest surprise was yet to come. When Papa came home he called us all down, and there in the carriage sat a brand new Singer sewing machine! Liza just had to hug someone when she saw it — she couldn't very well hug Papa — so she hugged Sarah and me. Then she very solemnly promised Papa he would never have cause to regret this investment.

Papa said he was quite sure that was true. He'd

ordered it just days after she came to live with us. "We're very lucky Mr. Smythe's shop is located on the other side of Bowrings so he was not burnt out. Ships have been coming so fast and thick, and he's able to get his orders in record time."

Liza couldn't take her eyes off the sewing machine while Mr. Morrissey took it down and sat it upright.

"It's a sin you'll have so little time to sew, with us being so busy in the shop and all," Phoebe said.

"Oh, but she will have time," Papa replied, and he told us he hopes to have at least half of our staff back at their old jobs soon, and most everyone before Christmas. He's even going make an offer on a space on Le Marchant Road for the candy kitchen. He turned to Liza and told her that Mrs. Steele will set up a workshop here as soon as a larger order of sewing machines can be obtained. "Until then, you'll be our seamstress," he concluded.

Ned and Papa carried the sewing machine upstairs, and Liza stayed at it until bedtime. The hideous mauve dress is now a dozen pincushions, stuffed with poor-box rags that were intended to clothe us. Sarah and Phoebe unpicked the lace from scraps of the dress by lamplight to make the trim. Mama and Papa are downstairs taking inventory and next week more shopgirls will return to their jobs. Even Patience and Prudence are coming back to work with Miss Rosy.

Wednesday, August 31st
Winsor & Son Mercantile Premises

Life is so dismal, it's almost as if bad luck came out of that poor box. Alfie comes home on Saturday, so of course time just drags by. If that weren't enough, it's been pouring rain all week. Trade is so slack that I'm actually writing in the shop while it's open! On Monday Papa only allowed Ned to make one trip across the harbour to post a notice to say our water cab service was suspended until the rain let up. Ned came back soaked to the skin, but undaunted by the weather. "People expects me to be there to bring them across to the shop now, Mr. Winsor," he told Papa. "They'll think I'm nothing but a useless hang-ashore when they sees I'm not coming."

This is the first time Ned has spoken up for himself, and I'm happy to see he's becoming his own person. I think Papa was pleased too, because he promised Ned a set of oilskins as soon as they can be found, so he can work in the rain.

So Ned isn't bringing customers across, people don't feel like carrying parcels in the soaking wet, and the roads on the South Side are, as Phoebe says, "some shocking muddy" for a place that's mostly rock. The only people we see are shop workers coming in to ask about their jobs. News spreads quickly in this town. Most of them don't even stop for a chat, rushing upstairs as if their jobs might run away.

Today Mama is taking down their particulars. Poor Papa had to go across to the north side in spite of the rain because he'd made an appointment to see a man about making a fence. (Municipal Council is making everyone fence off dangerous places now, and as our house is just a hole in the ground on Gower Street, it counts as a dangerous place.)

Sarah and Miss Rosy don't even notice the weather, devoting these rainy days to their hats. They are, as Liza says, on a tear, and soon we'll need a whole counter just for their work. Papa says we'll have a millinery department equal to that of the old store, and I think he's right. Which is fine for them, but not for me. I do wish something interesting would happen. The door just opened below, but it's probably only someone looking for work.

Wednesday evening

It wasn't one of Papa's crowd who came in when the door opened while I was writing, it was a policeman, asking for Papa. Sarah and I immediately offered to take the constable upstairs to Mama, we were so curious to know why he'd come. He introduced himself as Constable Harris and removed his helmet when he met Mama, but he wouldn't sit down. He asked, very politely, had we been the owners of a dwelling known as Windsor Castle?

Mama was taken aback. "Why, certainly not!"

The policeman realized he had misspoken and tried again. Surely we were the owners of that grand new house on Gower Street?

Mama agreed to this description.

"Well, Missus," he said, "we got some lot of furniture that folks took the liberty of 'saving' from that house the night of the fire." I could tell he knew they weren't *saving* things for us. "Some of it is in the Parade Street Rink, and some's in the old Drill Shed."

Mama was stunned into silence, so I asked, "What sort of property, Constable?"

He told us there was "every kind of thing. It's a bit of a joke among us," he added. "Seems like half the people who drag stuff in have something taken from — " he stopped himself just in time " — that grand house on Gower Street belonging to the Winsors." Then he told Mama that the Constabulary would be grateful if we'd come and claim it, adding that most people had already shown up to reclaim their property by now.

"We've been so busy setting up shop," Mama replied, "and you know, we felt sure everything was lost. To recover things now, almost two months after the fire — " She broke off in amazement.

Constable Harris smiled and told us this made a nice change "from all the grim tasks they have been at since the fire. Policing the lineups for relief, chasing after stolen goods and the people who claimed relief without the right to it." He said reuniting folks with things they thought were "gone to ashes" was a treat. Then he added, "You tell your good man to come along right quick." He glanced around the warehouse. "Spruce this place up like it's never been, all that fine furniture will."

Mama asked if he could stay to share the good news with Papa, but he said he was expected back at the station. Then Mama asked me to show the constable to the door. I did, then I rushed back up to the shop with the news. Sarah and I spent the evening trying to decide what we would most like to have again. I want my bed back, but Sarah thinks it unlikely we'll recover anything so big. I did not argue with her, but if someone could steal a piano while the fire closed in, surely it would be possible to steal a four-poster bed.

To think we may see our furniture again!

Thursday, September 1st
Winsor & Son Mercantile Premises

It's still raining. Papa says he can only spare the time to go look for our furniture once, and there's no point in going in the rain because the police would very likely load everything into a cart immediately and the varnish on the furniture would be ruined, so we must wait for better weather. My whole life is one big wait this week.

Today while Sarah and Miss Rosy worked on their hats and Liza sewed, Phoebe and I loitered at the counters waiting for customers. Phoebe was looking through *The Evening Telegram* (which has finally begun to publish again, with a new press that just arrived from New York). She came upon a story so interesting she had to tell us about it. "Listen here. A young domestic left the island to find work, like people kept telling us we should," she said to Liza and Miss Rosy. "On the boat to Halifax, she met a man who'd come home from Seattle, Washington, to see about his people after the fire. It was love at first sight. They got married right there in Halifax. Just imagine, she left St. John's penniless and now she's the wife of a wealthy man. It says her new husband is worth more than $15,000."

Miss Rosy asked who she was.

"Miss Struggles, it says."

I giggled and Liza frowned. "Somebody's after making that story up, Phoebe," she said, adding that there's never been anyone by the name of Struggles in St. John's.

Phoebe defended the story, noting that it had been taken right out of *The Halifax Herald*, and even included the name of the minister who'd married them. "You think they manufacture the news over there in Halifax?" she demanded. Then she sighed. "Just think, that could have been one of us."

Liza asked where Seattle, Washington, was. Miss Rosy told her it was near Vancouver. "I'm glad it wasn't one of us," she added. "I don't wish Miss Struggles any grief, but she'll always be beholden to that man for raising her up like that, won't she? And you can't trust a wealthy man. I only wish I'd learned that sooner." She didn't look up while she spoke, pinning ribbon so savagely it made me feel sorry for the hat.

Thankfully, Nettie chose that moment to bring us tea and raisin buns. As she put the teapot down, I saw Liza and Phoebe exchange a look, and I was shocked to find they pity Miss Rosy. Even though she is beautiful and clever, her life is in ruins.

Nettie was a good distraction, with plenty to say about the furniture. She would like a proper kitchen cupboard, so she can stop putting dishes into filthy old crates. Sarah would like to see our china cabinet again, so Mama's wedding china and silver would have "a proper place to stay."

I think it's noble of her to want something for Mama most of all. I still long for my bed.

Friday, September 2nd
Winsor & Son Mercantile Premises

The sun has finally shown itself again, so we can hope that Alfie's voyage home will be a pleasant one, but all this waiting must be having a bad effect on me. I had such a terrible dream last night, and it still clings to me like cobwebs on my face. We were on the north side, meeting Alfie, just as we will tomorrow. He came down the gangplank with Ruby, but he didn't notice me at all. When Papa took us all for ice cream (as he plans to do), Alfie only wanted to sit with Ruby. He'd forgotten all about me. The dream was so vivid when I woke up, I was convinced it was real. Only when I saw Alfie's bed, made up and ready for him, did I realize it was a dream. Alfie will be home tomorrow and I wonder, might my dream come true?

Papa has hired back so many shopgirls now, I am no longer needed (and Sarah and I start back to school again next week in any case). This day is going to drag.

Friday evening

I was wrong about the day. When I finished writing, Mama proposed an outing. She may have been trying to keep her mind off the furniture that is waiting for us *still*. Today Papa had to visit some cabinetmakers in the west end who are going to build fine new cupboards and counters so we can get clear of all these packing crates. In time these furnishings will be moved into our new store.

There was a crate of canning jars in with all the new housewares, and Mama said we could make good use of our mountain of sugar by picking blueberries for jam. The South Side hills are covered in blueberry bushes. When Mr. Matt learned we were going berry picking, he offered to accompany us. He has taken two weeks off, and tomorrow he's sailing home to Trinity to visit his family. (When he returns, he will bring all the tinsmithing tools he needs to resume working for us again.) So he was at loose ends too, just waiting to leave. Mama even prevailed upon Sarah to take an hour away from her hats so we could have a proper outing.

Nettie found some tin bowls for berries and packed bread and molasses for a lunch, and off we went. We found a drung that led between two gardens into the barrens high above the houses. I could look right down on the roof of our warehouse and see the saucy seagulls perched on it.

We spread out to hunt for berries, and I soon found myself at a good patch, seated near Mr. Matt. Mama and Sarah were not too distant, but out of earshot. Berry picking is a grand way to pass an afternoon and I should have been happy, but I couldn't shake the heaviness that bad dream had laid upon me, so my bowl filled slowly.

Mr. Matt noticed. "Triffie my maid, you're dragging your tail feathers today. What's wrong?"

"Alfie's been gone so long. What if he's forgotten me?"

Mr. Matt laughed, but not in a mean way, reminding me Alfie hasn't been gone for two months. "Do you imagine he'd forget you in so short a time?"

I said that so much has happened, it seems like years.

"And you still find fault with Ruby for taking him away, do you?" he asked.

I stopped picking and sighed. "Ruby was trying to be good. I know that now. I hope, when she comes back, I will be good enough to forgive her, but it may be beyond me."

I expected the kind of moralizing lecture that adults are bound to give at such moments, but Mr. Matt surprised me. "Fair enough," he said. "Guaranteed I know how that feels."

We picked on in silence. Until then, I had thought he was just angry with Miss Rosy. It never occurred to me that he might wish to forgive her, but find himself unable to. I spent a long moment of careful thought before I spoke again. "She's very sorry she threw you over," I said at last. My voice was quiet, so Mr. Matt could pretend he hadn't heard me if he wanted.

His jaw dropped. "How would you know such a thing?"

"Everyone knows," I told him. "You never look at her, so you don't see."

"Out of the mouths of babes," he said. He picked a few handfuls of berries, then he said, "You've given me a lot to think on, Triffie my maid."

That was all. I couldn't help hoping it would change everything, that Mr. Matt would come back from berry picking and sweep Miss Rosy off her feet. I've always wanted to see what that would look like, but it didn't happen. Instead Mr. Matt went off to Fort Amherst to see if he could buy some cod for supper. Tomorrow Alfie and Ruby come home and Mr. Matt leaves. If he's not able to forgive, how can I?

Sunday, September 4th, Home

When I look at the lovely row of jars filled with jam, it seems hard to believe how sad I was when we picked the blueberries. On Saturday morning, everyone was too excited to notice my apprehension. Liza and Ned had never tasted ice cream before, so they were mainly looking forward to the treat. As they'd never met Alfie, no one could blame them. Mama hummed as she straightened the old quilt on Alfie's bed at least a hundred times, and then she'd hug Sarah, or Papa, or me, whoever happened to be nearest, every minute or two. I placed all Alfie's tin soldiers at his bedside table.

When dinner was finally over, Mama said, "We had better get into our Sunday clothes now."

"The *Prince Le Boo* isn't really royalty, Mrs. Winsor," Mr. Matt joked.

Mama smiled. "Professor Danielle isn't royalty either, but you'd never know it. His restaurant's only that little shed of a place at Beck's Cove now, but he still calls it The Royal and I'm sure he's just as likely as ever to ask you to leave if your manners don't suit him."

Nettie remarked it was a wonder he'd never learned humility, as this was the second time in his life he'd been burnt out.

None of this talk was helping Ned. "Perhaps I'd do best to wait with the rodney," he mumbled.

"Ned Shamler, don't you dare!" Mama replied.

"Sure," Liza said, "I got that suit from London fixed up so fine, everyone's going to think the Winsors have been hiding their older son away."

"Maybe you was off to England, getting a fine education to go with that suit," Phoebe teased.

Mama allowed that Ned could handle a spoon as well as any of us, and that was that. Then we all went to get ready.

Sarah and I went into our little packing-crate dressing closet to change. I pulled my rose satin dress over my head, remembering the horrible mauve dress from London, all spattered with tea stains. Professor Danielle would stop a dress like that at his door. It was true, what Mama said that day, "Not all charity is kind."

As Sarah did up my buttons for me and tied the sash, another dress popped into my mind — the scratchy wool one I'd given Ruby last Boxing Day, which now seemed like a hundred years ago.

Just now I stopped writing to leaf back through this book so I could read exactly what I thought when I first started this diary. *Those who are unfortunate enough to be poor should at least have the grace to show gratitude.* My words could have been written by a stranger, a girl I'd never want for a friend. I knew that dress was itchy, I knew it wasn't pretty, and I burn with shame to see how annoyed I'd been with Ruby for failing to seem properly grateful. She'd had no one to tell her she could cast that dress aside, no one to make it into pincushions for her. She was stuck with my unkind charity.

But I must swallow my shame and continue with my story.

When Sarah and I joined the others, Papa remarked that we are now a more respectable looking crew than we were in the weeks after the fire. Liza puts her sewing machine to good use, so even the hand-me-downs from their days in the park fit smartly now, but on Saturday Phoebe, Liza and Miss Rosy were decked out in their finest. Miss Rosy wore a midnight blue velvet hat trimmed with white satin roses. The brim was so wide, her face was mostly hidden, and I thought that a shame, because Mr. Matt might want to take a better look at her now. It seemed clear he had no intention of sweeping her off her feet, and I wondered if she would be doomed to live with a broken heart forever.

When we'd all piled into the rodney, Mr. Matt and Ned took the oars together. "I won't be here to help you row back again," Mr. Matt said. He had a little valise with him. Sarah and I were in the prow with Miss Rosy. Mr. Matt and Ned faced away from us.

"I've been known to put my hand to an oar from time to time," Papa said.

Then Mama told Mr. Matt she didn't see how anyone could go away for two weeks with such a small case. She was laughing when she said this.

"Oh, Mother'll have new clothes waiting when I gets there," he replied. "I'll need a bigger one for the trip back." Then he and Ned began to row in earnest and they fell silent.

The city slowly got closer. When I look at it now, all the lost and ruined buildings rise in my mind's eye — the Athenaeum, the Kirk and pretty Ashton Cottage where I told May I would live when I grow up, and our school just up the hill, all gone. The very city I imagined I'd live in when I grow up is gone. New buildings of unpainted, raw lumber sprout among the ruins now. Most are just shanties, but a few are built to last.

Mr. Matt drew our attention to a vessel that had just sailed through the Narrows. "That might well be the *Prince Le Boo*." The ship was far away, but it came steadily closer and soon I could make out a small boy and a girl with red hair standing by the rail.

"Look, you can see Alfie," I cried, standing up. The rodney's a stable boat, so nothing happened, but Miss Rosy took me by the hand and very firmly sat me down again.

"Try to keep yourself out of the harbour, dear," Mama said. "That's still your one good dress." Everyone laughed because I was never in danger of falling in.

Alfie didn't see us. The rodney is small and he would have expected us to meet him with a carriage. The *Prince Le Boo* sailed steadily toward the wharf at Clift's Cove where we knew it would dock. Ned brought the rodney into Beck's Cove and everyone scrambled out from the back of the boat, until only Sarah, Miss Rosy and I were left. Papa helped Sarah up, then he said, "Up you come, Triffie. I'm not about to risk having you fall in." The others were already walking to Water Street, but I waited while Papa joined Mama. Miss Rosy was the only one left now. She looked up at Mr. Matt and her face was as blank as a sheet of paper. After all these weeks of silence, she expected nothing from him now.

"Rose," he said, "will you give me your hand?" He extended his to her.

Her smile was like the sun coming out on a gloomy day. It seemed as if all the colour poured back into her world. "Thank you, Matthew," she replied. "I would be happy to," and he helped her out of the boat. They walked away not touching, but with their heads together like two people who had a great deal to say to one another. I think they had forgotten all about me, so I scooted past and caught up with Mama, who took my hand in hers.

It's a short walk from Beck's Cove to Clift's Cove, and the *Prince Le Boo* was putting out her gangplank when we arrived. Alfie had changed so much! He was brown as a berry with hair bleached almost white by the sun and he looked so strong and healthy. As soon as his turn came, he ran down the gangplank and straight into my arms. "Triffie! I've been gone so long. Did you miss me?"

I hugged him tight. "Every day."

Papa swept him up and Mama hugged him and Papa together, then he was passed to Sarah. Ruby stood there on the wharf, alone and unnoticed. Her plain brown dress looked new and homemade. I wondered what it must be like for her, leaving her family to come back to this strange new life of ours.

While Alfie prattled on about his summer and all the fun he'd had — jigging off the wharf, feeding the chickens, making bonfires on the beach — I went over to Ruby. "Looks as if your crowd took good care of him," I said. "Welcome back. Everything's different, but we're getting used to it." I told her that Papa was treating us all to ice cream and she was invited. Then I offered to introduce her to everyone she hadn't met.

Ruby's smile told me that she could see things really were different.

Professor Danielle seated us himself in The Royal and, if we'd only closed our eyes, we could have imagined his little shed was a palace. And Mama was right, the fire hadn't changed him at all. He was eyeing Ruby's homemade dress as she sat beside me in my good rose satin, but before he could say anything, I gave him a look and he suddenly remembered he had other customers to mind. Everyone else was busy with their menus, so only Mama saw. Later, she told Sarah I could have stopped a clock with that look, but she said this in a most approving way.

Ruby and Alfie seem exhausted by their summer. Both fell asleep early last night and they're already sound asleep now. Mr. Matt is gone, but Miss Rosy isn't sad. She's asked if she can borrow my writing desk, and I believe she will be writing to Trinity. Sarah and I start school tomorrow, and Papa still hasn't found the time to see about our furniture!

Wednesday, September 7th, Home

I am writing at our dining-room table! We only recovered half the chairs, but that doesn't matter. Our attic is transformed by all the fine furniture. But even before the furniture arrived, Monday began like Christmas for me. I was resigned to going back to school in my worn out everyday dress, but when

I woke, I found a lovely new dress lying on the quilt! It's made of forest-green poplin, and almost feels too rich for everyday wear. Mama and Liza planned the surprise together. Liza "borrowed" my rose satin one night while I was asleep to get my measurements, working late hours to finish it. It is perfection and I felt like a little queen when I left the warehouse.

Papa engaged Mr. Morrissey to take us over in his carriage so we wouldn't have to walk from a wharf to school our first day. (Though it's only a few blocks from the harbour and we have been walking since.) I think Ned might have been put out by Papa's decision if not for Alfie, who was staying home because his school didn't open until yesterday. As soon as they met, Alfie seemed to decide Ned is exactly the person he would like to be one day, and he's rarely from his side. I'm not jealous. It will do Ned a world of good to have someone looking up to him for a change, and I have love enough in my life that I can spare a bit of Alfie's.

It still feels strange to be with all the other girls in this old schoolhouse (which still gives off a smell of empty neglect). So many of the girls were in dresses that are worse for wear, I was almost embarrassed by my good fortune. (I had to explain to Mama and Liza why I chose to wear my old cotton calico today.) But May and I have been promoted to Class III! Now, we have Miss Lily Simms for our teacher. She only graduated herself a few years ago and has a very pretty smile, which she's not afraid to show in class. I've watched for Susie Verge to see if she'd be back at school with us but, so far, she hasn't appeared. I heard they've opened a school in the park and I wonder if she'll be staying there. I hope not. She's so clever, she deserves to be in a good school.

Sarah and I came home after school to find the shop humming, but Mama and Papa were nowhere to be seen, and Nettie told us they had finally gone to see about the furniture, taking lucky Alfie with them! We could only wait outside to watch for wagons, and soon three appeared! I ran for Nettie.

There was a wagonload of smaller things, and two filled with furniture. "My bed!" I cried, and then I paused. "Or perhaps it's Sarah's."

Sarah replied that it hardly mattered, since we'll be sharing the bed, whoever it belonged to, but Papa said not just yet, as Mama would not allow the mattress home.

Mama's noise wrinkled. "Heaven knows what vermin it might hold now. I told the constables to burn it."

"Oh, look," Sarah cried. "The china cabinet!" And Mama, pointing underneath, drew Nettie's attention to the kitchen cupboard. Papa called for Ned, and soon we were all carrying things upstairs. The heavier pieces went up through the loophole under Ned's careful direction. Alfie was agog to see how well he handled everything.

We are grateful to the police, of course, but I feel oddly thankful for the many looters who emptied our house while the fire raged. And Mouser, who played a role, I allow, for Mama would have locked the door without her. And Alfie's weak chest. As I write, I can picture people grabbing things and rushing away as the fire loomed ever closer. Almost everything came from the first floor. Of all the upstairs furniture, only that one bed survived. In the end, Sarah and I decided it should go to Mama and Papa rather than ourselves.

The china cabinet looks the same as ever, except a pane of glass in the hutch is gone. The good china sparkles inside, and I'm sure it must be glad to be home again. The dining-room table looks only a bit strange with our barrel chairs around it. Best of all, the parlour carpet is back. It's a fine Turkey carpet in a Tree of Life design worked in pretty colours — navy and red and gold. Sometimes, when no one is looking, I slip my shoes and stockings off and wiggle my toes in it.

All of Mama's wedding crystal is gone, and so is her pottery and glass collection, except for one blue glass vase. Mama has placed it on her whatnot, which once held a dozen or more of its kind. Today, she just sat looking at it and I thought she was missing all the others until Sarah put her arms around Mama's neck and said, "I wish you still hadn't lost so many, Mama."

She kissed Sarah and smiled. "You know," she replied, "I believe I value this one vase now more than I did the whole collection, back when we had so much."

And that might sound strange, but as she spoke I caught sight of my forest-green poplin on the hook above my bed, glowing in a shaft of late sunlight. I knew that no dress would ever be more beautiful to me and I believe I understand exactly how Mama feels.

Epilogue

Like many St. John's merchants, Triffie's father was able to weather the economic depression caused by the bank crash of 1894 and his store continued, even though many employees in all walks of life lost their jobs and left Newfoundland for New York, Boston or Toronto. Sarah graduated from school when she was sixteen and, a few years later, became engaged to a young lawyer. They had a long and happy marriage, and Triffie loved her little nieces and nephews dearly.

Alfie and Ned both volunteered to join the Newfoundland Regiment when World War I broke out in 1914. Alfie was rejected because of his asthma, and went to work in his father's shop when he gradu-ated from the Church of England Academy, which by then was called Bishop Feild College. Just before Ned left to fight in France, he married Susie Verge, whom he met the Christmas after the fire when she was living in Bannerman Park. He was wounded in the Battle of the Somme on July 1st, 1916, and lay on the battlefield for three days, convinced he was dying, before he was rescued and eventually returned to Newfoundland. Mr. Winsor, and Alfie after him, always found a place for Ned in the family business. When Ned's wounded leg made it impossible for him to do active work, he learned to be a bookkeeper.

Matthew Bright and Rose Noseworthy married in the summer of 1893. When the bank crash made life difficult in St. John's, they relocated to his native town of Trinity. For decades after, a hat made by Mrs. Rose Bright was considered essential for the well-dressed woman on any major occasion, all the way from Trinity Bay North to Bonavista Bay South. They named their first daughter Tryphena.

Triffie's drawing talents increased as she grew and she studied art at the St. John's Art School under the direction of John Nichols, the drawing master who visited the Synod Girls' School. A few suitors proposed, but she rejected them all. By the time Mr. Nichols retired in 1908, Triffie began to give private drawing lessons and everyone in her family regarded her as a confirmed old maid. That year, she attended a lecture given by an American doctor, Robert Broadmore, who had visited Labrador as a medical missionary. Attracted by her clever questions, he asked if they might correspond by letter. Two years later, when he returned to St. John's, he proposed. Triffie accepted and her dream of travelling the world was finally realized. She continued to sketch even after her two sons were born, and her views of exotic places, from Labrador to India and many places between, were proudly displayed on walls in all her friends' houses.

St. John's has never had another fire like the one in 1892.

Historical Note

In January of 1890, a visitor from New York described St. John's, Newfoundland, like this: "Upset a child's box of toy houses down a very steep hillside, overturn a mud cart on top of them, [and] send a good hard shower of rain to mix all these ingredients well up together." The city may have seemed quaint and backward to him, but St. John's was proudly modern. A water system piped clean water into homes, a gasworks provided light and there was even a new electricity plant. Safe behind the massive rock hills that protect St. John's from the open sea, this harbour town of about thirty thousand people was thriving. Then, suddenly, everything changed.

St. John's had seen many fires before, and after the last big fire in 1846, streets were widened and no wooden buildings were allowed on the two main downtown thoroughfares of Water and Duckworth Streets. The city had a system of water tanks, three fire stations — each equipped with a huge fire bell — and a modern steam-powered fire engine. People felt confident their city was safe from fire.

To lose two-thirds of a city overnight to fire, many things must go wrong. On July 8, 1892, everything went wrong. The weather had been unusually hot and dry for weeks, so the wooden houses were completely dry. Strong winds gusted over the city toward the sea, whipping up waves in the harbour, and the water supply had been shut off for the day to make repairs to the pipes. The water was turned on again by 4:00 p.m., but it would take hours to reach the upper levels of the city.

Around 4:30 p.m. some farm helpers were busy milking cows in a large barn on Freshwater Road, uphill from the harbour, when one of them dropped his pipe or a match into a pile of hay. A bucket of water would have put the fire out, but there was no water. Firefighters soon arrived to find the barn and adjoining house in flames. About 9 metres from the barn stood a tank intended to provide water for fighting fires, but it had been emptied weeks before when the firemen were practising, and had not been refilled. The firefighters were helpless.

High winds swept burning debris down the hill toward the harbour, and soon small fires sprang up all over the downtown. Before an hour had passed, people realized their terrible situation and began to leave their houses, taking whatever they could. Many put possessions and property into sturdy brick and stone buildings downtown, such as the Anglican Cathedral, and gathered upwind in Bannerman Park, on the grounds nearby Government House, or near the Catholic Cathedral. Even though crews of men tried to fight the fires, everything worked against them. The fire burned all night. By morning, over a thousand houses and most of the downtown business district were gone. Out of the thirty thousand people who lived in the city, just over ten thousand were now homeless.

News was sent by telegraph to the rest of the world. Big fires were not unusual in cities in the 1800s, and people all over North America and Britain responded with generosity. The first aid — tents and blankets and food — arrived from Halifax by ship just days after the fire.

Most people found shelter with relatives or friends, or built sheds of their own, sometimes in the ruins of their own houses, but about fifteen hundred people had nowhere to go. Sheds were built for them in Bannerman Park and on Parade Street near the Constabulary barracks at Fort Townsend. They were built so quickly, they had no floors. People rented these sheds for $25 a year; more than a year after the fire, some were still living in them. Others spent that first summer in tents on the shore of Quidi Vidi Lake.

Streets in the downtown were widened and straightened again after the 1892 fire. The spot where Triffie's school once stood is now in the middle of a road. Like Triffie's family, the merchants of St. John's recovered quickly, but it took about three years before the city was fully restored. The many theatres that had attracted travelling companies from the United States and Britain never recovered. Some cultural landmarks, such as the huge City Hall Skating Rink and the Athenaeum, were lost forever. Then in 1894 a bank crash plunged Newfoundland into an economic depression and St. John's was never quite the glittering Victorian city of Triffie's childhood again.

Glossary

at sixes and sevens: out of sorts; confused

barachois: spit of land and pond near Freshwater Bay

between the jigs and the reels: in the middle of everything

bread soda: baking soda

brin bag: burlap bag

buckram: heavy cotton cloth

clewed up: finished

close: stuffy

crossing-sweeper boy: street urchin

crowd: group of closely-related people

a dab hand: handy

drung: laneway

flankers: large cinders

galey: the state cats get into when the wind is high

hangashore: layabout; lazy person

have the vapours: a nervous condition of women in Victorian times

jigging: fishing

jink: jinx

like a birch broom in the fits: messy hair

lunch: a snack

mauzy: cool and foggy

now the once: right now

peppermint knob: peppermint candy

playing copyhouses/cobbyhouses: playing house

rodney: small seaworthy boat

sleeveen: thug or rogue

some: very, as in "some ugly"

streeling: dragging; moving in a disorderly way

think on: think about

tilt: shelter, lean-to, hut

wincey: linsey-woolsey, wool and cotton fabric used for clothing

Where's he to?: Where is he?

wonderful sad: very sad

yaffle: armload

The S.S. Miranda, St. John's Harbour, around 1885. Merchant premises Harvey and Company and March and Sons are fore and aft. The City Hall Skating Rink is at the upper left.

Water Street before the fire. St. John's natural harbour is protected from the open Atlantic by the Narrows. On the right is the edge of the South Side neighbourhood, where many relocated after the fire.

The busy wharves of St. John's Harbour were turned into charred stumps by the fire.

Because coal was stored inside them, many buildings smoked for days after the fire. The ruin of Ordnance House is on the right.

The 1892 fire caused over $13 million in property damage. Many buildings were reduced to piles of rubble.

Water Street stores became gutted shells.

People without places to stay had to live in temporary shelters known as "tilts" in Bannerman Park for months.

The ruins of the Anglican Cathedral (centre, top) and Gower Street Methodist Church overlook crumbled walls and foundations of the Methodist College and Masonic Temple.

ST. JOHN'S, N.F., IN FLAMES

Over 150 Buildings Destroyed When Communication Was Cut Off.

MANY PEOPLE DESTITUTE

**Some of the Most Prominent Edifices
Burned and the Fire Sweeping
All Before It—An Appeal
for Aid.**

HALIFAX, July 8.—Reports from St. John's, Nfld, say that a fire broke out about 4 o'clock this afternoon in a house on Long's Hill, in the rear of the town. A strong gale of wind from the southwest was prevailing at the time and the flames spread very rapidly across the town, sweeping everything before them.

Owing to the telegraph office having to be deserted early in the evening it is impossible to get full particulars, but it is thought the city will be almost completely wiped out.

Among the buildings destroyed are the Church of England cathedral, Masonic temple, Orange hall, Atheneum, Methodist church and college, Roman Catholic cathedral and palace, St. Patrick's hall, the Kirk, Atlantic hotel, Linberg's brewery and the Commercial and Union Bank.

News of the fire spread across the Commonwealth, including neighbouring Canada, as reported in Montreal's The Gazette *on July 9, 1892. The article is not completely accurate — the Roman Catholic Cathedral and the Union Bank were not destroyed.*

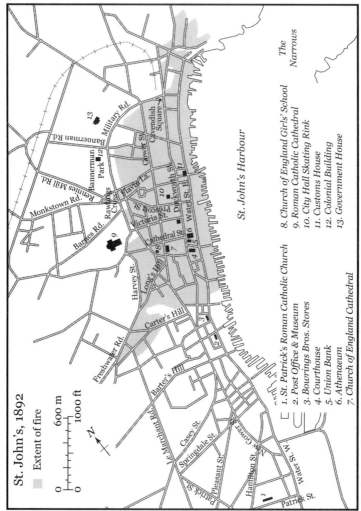

St. John's, 1892

Extent of fire

0 600 m
0 1000 ft

N

St. John's Harbour

The Narrows

1. St. Patrick's Roman Catholic Church
2. Post Office & Museum
3. Bowrings Bros. Stores
4. Courthouse
5. Union Bank
6. Athenaeum
7. Church of England Cathedral
8. Church of England Girls' School
9. Roman Catholic Cathedral
10. City Hall Skating Rink
11. Customs House
12. Colonial Building
13. Government House

Military Rd.
Bannerman Rd.
Rennies Mill Rd.
Monkstown Rd.
Barnes Rd.
Harvey St.
Freshwater Rd.
Carter's Hill
Barter's Hill
Casey St.
Springdale St.
Hamilton St.
Le Marchant Rd.
New Gower St.
Water St. W.
Pleasant St.
Patrick St.
Patrick St.
Long's Hill
Rawlin's Cross
Victoria St.
Prescott St.
Cathedral St.
Flavin La.
Cower St.
Cavendish Square
Dicksworth St.
Water St. E.
Bannerman Park

The fire started along Freshwater Road and spread quickly. Most of St. John's downtown was destroyed by the fire, though few people were killed in the blaze.

188

Credits

Cover cameo (detail): *A Little Girl*, Cecilia Beaux; image courtesy of the Art Renewal Center® www.artrenewal.org.

Cover background (detail): *Downtown St. John's after the fire*, 8 August 1892; photographer S.H. Parsons; reproduced by permission of Archives and Special Collections (Coll.-137, file no. 05.01.007), Queen Elizabeth II Library, Memorial University, St. John's, NL.

Page 179: *S.S.* Miranda *with view of the city in the background: Harvey and Company premises and March and Sons premises, c. 1885*; reproduced by permission of Archives and Special Collections, Queen Elizabeth II Library, Memorial University, St. John's, NL (Coll-137, file no. 3.05.012).

Page 180: *View of south side of Water Street and Sclater's Store, pre-1892;* reproduced by permission of Archives and Special Collections, Queen Elizabeth II Library, Memorial University, St. John's, NL; Coll-137, file no. 1.02.005.

Page 181: *1892 Fire, St. John's. View looking west from the railway track, showing Devon row and the harbour, in the aftermath of the 1892 fire;* reproduced by permission of Archives and Special Collections, Queen Elizabeth II Library, Memorial University, St. John's, NL; Coll-137, file no. 05.01.012.

Page 182. *St. John's after the fire, still smouldering [after 8 July, 1892]*, S.H. Parsons; The Rooms Provincial Archives Division, VA-152-46.

Page 183: *Ruins After the Great Fire, ca. July-August 1892;* reproduced by permission of Archives and Special Collections, Queen Elizabeth II Library, Memorial University, St. John's, NL; Coll-137, file no. 05.01.008.

Page 184: *Water Street stores in ruins, ca. July-August 1892*; reproduced by permission of Archives and Special Collections, Queen Elizabeth II Library, Memorial University, St. John's, NL; Coll-137, file no. 05.01.011.

Page 185: *Tilts put up in the Park to shelter the poor who had been burnt out*, Eliot Curwen, Eliot Curwen fonds, The Rooms Provincial Archives Division, VA 152-53.

Page 186: *View of the Anglican Cathedral of St. John the Baptist which was burned by the fire of 1892;* Library and Archives Canada, PA-066621.

Page 187: reproduced from item in Montreal's *The Gazette*, July 9, 1892.

Page 188: Map copyright © Paul Heersink/Paperglyphs.

In memory of Paul O'Neill (1928–2013)
actor, broadcaster, historian of St. John's,
kindly employer, bon vivant.

About the Author

Janet McNaughton has a doctorate in folklore, so it's not surprising that she loves digging into research, where she sometimes finds things that surprise her. "The people who wrote eyewitness accounts of the great fire of 1892 almost never mentioned the looting that went on while the fire raged, but stories of raids and arrests crept into the local newspapers soon after. Stores on Water Street were completely emptied; and furniture and carpets — even a piano — disappeared from some houses. I expected that people would be tried and put in jail, and even went looking for court records.

"Although some people were charged at first, the authorities must soon have realized that Her Majesty's Penitentiary would not be big enough to hold all offenders. One day near the end of July 1892, police collected two cartloads of stolen furniture in the neighbourhood where I now live, without arresting anyone. By August, the newspapers ran a regular notice, telling people to surrender what they had stolen or face the consequences. Soon the police had recovered enough things to fill a curling rink and an old military parade shed. I was surprised at first to learn that so many people were not punished for a crime as serious as looting, but Newfoundlanders are practical and forgiving. This way, people who had acted badly in the heat of the moment could make amends, while those who lost their houses were unexpectedly reunited with some of their lost valuables."

Though she was born in Toronto, Janet has lived in St. John's, Newfoundland, for thirty-five years — her current home is not so very far from where the 1892 fire started. As she walks the city, she now envisions the streets as they were over a century ago. "It's as if an old plate glass photo negative of the city before the fire appears in my imagination when I look at St. John's. I can see the modern city I've always known, but now I also see many of the buildings that disappeared overnight in July of 1892. I wasn't expecting this book to change the way I look at my home city, but it certainly did."

One thing Janet loves as much as research is reading . . . though that has also got her into trouble. She says that as a child in grade two she grew to love where stories would take her. In fact, she loved reading so much, and spent so much time at it, her parents actually took away her library card.

Janet's novels, including *To Dance at the Palais Royale, The Secret Under My Skin* and *Make or Break Spring,* have won the Geoffrey Bilson Award for Historical Fiction, the Ann Connor Brimer Award, the Violet Downey IODE Award, a Canadian Library Association Book of the Year Honour Book and a Mr. Christie's Book Award, among many others.

Acknowledgements

Many people helped with this book, and I would like to thank them. Joan Ritcey, head of the Centre for Newfoundland Studies, and Linda White from the CNS Archives both patiently dealt with my questions, even the ones that had no immediate answer. The CNS also borrowed the only existing hard copies of *The Morning Despatch*, and had them scanned and posted in the Memorial University Library's digital archive collection, making my work much, much easier than it would have been otherwise.

Helen Miller and her staff at the St. John's City Archives gave me hours of their time, helping to locate and name houses and buildings that disappeared in the fire of 1892. Dr. Philip Hiscock of the Folklore Department at Memorial University was always available to discuss the fine points of Newfoundland English, and actor and children's author Andy Jones helped me nail down the elusive cod of misery.

Two dear writing friends got this book off to a proper start. Barbara Haworth-Attard was brave enough to tell me that Triffie, in her earliest version, was not a likable character. Karleen Bradford later confirmed that Barb's advice had set me on the right path. My agent, Ginger Clark, then picked up the ball and ran with it to Scholastic, a publisher that has far exceeded my expectations. I want to thank fact checker Barbara Hehner and Dr. Melvin Baker of Memorial University's History Department for asking all the right questions and saving me from embarrassing mistakes. Finally, Sandy Bogart Johnston has been an insightful editor who was extremely easy to work with, and Diane Kerner's input was always valuable. I felt I was in good hands while working on this book.

Copyright © 2014 by Janet McNaughton

All rights reserved. Published by Scholastic Canada Ltd.
SCHOLASTIC and DEAR CANADA and logos are trademarks
and/or registered trademarks of Scholastic Inc.

www.scholastic.ca

Library and Archives Canada Cataloguing in Publication

McNaughton, Janet, 1953-, author
Flame and ashes : the Great Fire diary of Triffie
Winsor / Janet McNaughton.

(Dear Canada)
Issued in print and electronic formats.
ISBN 978-1-4431-2443-0 (bound).--ISBN 978-1-4431-3901-4 (html)

I. Title. II. Series: Dear Canada

PS8575.N385F53 2014   jC813'.54   C2014-901801-0
                         C2014-901802-9

6 5 4 3 2 1   Printed in Canada   114   14 15 16 17 18

First printing September 2014

Go to www.scholastic.ca/dearcanada for information on the
Dear Canada series — see inside the books, read an excerpt
or a review, post a review, and more.